TO
VEX
A
Viscount

COPYRIGHT

To Vex a Viscount
Lords of London, Book 4
Copyright © 2018 by Tamara Gill
Cover Art by Wicked Smart Designs
Editor Authors Designs
Editor Free Bird Editing
All rights reserved.

ISBN-13: 978-0-6484133-3-2
ISBN-10: 0-6484133-3-0

DEDICATION

For my friend, Serena Clarke.
Thank you.

PROLOGUE

J. Smith & Sons Solicitors, London, August 1812

Lord Hugo Blythe, fourth Viscount Wakely, stared mutely at his solicitor of many years, Mr. Thompson. He blinked, fighting to comprehend the meaning behind the gentleman's words.

Damn my father to hell. Had he not already been dead, Hugo might have killed him himself for playing such a game.

"I'm sorry, but can you explain to me again what the terms are of my father's will? I'm not sure it's making sense to me. You said I must marry within a year? This part I'm a little muddled about." How he dearly wished there really was some confusion on his part.

Mr. Thompson, a stout older gentleman with a receding hairline but honest features, threw him a pitying glance and then stared down at the paperwork before him again.

"The will explains that as per your birthright, you inherit the title of viscount, and Bolton Abbey, along with the London home and the estate in Cumbria and Ireland.

However, the dowry your mother brought to the family upon her marriage to your father will revert to her family should you not marry by your thirtieth birthday. I believe that is less than twelve months away."

Disbelief sat in Hugo's gut like a heavy boulder. "Only just. July twenty-third, to be exact," he said, running a hand over his jaw. How could his father do this to him? Of course, they'd had many discussions—very well, arguments—about his dallying and raking about town without any direction toward marriage, but to do this to him, forcing his hand, was beyond cruel.

His solicitor placed down his papers and met his gaze. "I suggest that you find a wife before the end of the next season. If you fail to satisfy that clause, the money will go to your uncle in New York according to your father's instructions. Your uncle has been notified of this condition and is receptive to claiming the money that went with his sister to your father upon their marriage. The clause is quite watertight and cannot be waived. Of course, looking at the financial statements regarding your inheritance, should you lose this money, there will be very little remaining to keep the estates running. You may have to look to leasing them out indefinitely, as you're unable to sell due to them being entailed properties."

A weight settled on Hugo's shoulders and he slumped back in his chair, not having known it was as bad as all that. "Did Father state exactly who I'm to marry?" He'd certainly spoken loudly enough from beyond the grave with his will, he might as well also state who was acceptable.

"As to that…" Mr. Thompson said, shifting on his seat and looking a little uncomfortable for the first time during their meeting.

The weight on Hugo's shoulders doubled.

"Your father has stipulated that not only are you to marry before your thirtieth birthday, but you are also required to marry a woman of fortune, as he did. No less than thirty thousand pounds must be her dowry. Your father wrote that he asks this of you to ensure that the family name, and all those who rely on your lands for their livelihood, are kept secure. He also wrote that he believes you are more than capable of this task, and he wishes you well and every happiness in your future marriage."

Hugo met his solicitor's gaze, unable to fathom what he was being told. He'd thought he would have more time before he settled down. He very much enjoyed being an eligible bachelor, but the select, very scandalous house parties that he was accustomed to would all have to stop if he were to find a wife. How dull. A wife. His life was over.

Mr. Thompson stood, holding out a rolled-up copy of the will tied with dark pink ribbon. Hugo clasped it, the urge to scrunch it up into a ball of rubbish being his first thought.

"Good luck, Lord Wakely. If you have any further questions, please do not hesitate to call on me. I'm at your disposal whenever you need."

Hugo shook his hand, then, swiping up his hat and gloves, strode for the door. "Thank you, sir. Once I have found the poor victim who will become my wife, I shall be in contact."

And she would be a victim, for a marriage made in haste, and solely due to requiring funds, would never be a good match. He'd always admired the love match marriages of the couples with whom he associated, knowing he too would desire such a connection for himself. Just not yet.

He stopped on the cobbled pavement and slammed his beaver hat on his head. *Damn.* If what the solicitor said was true, and there was no doubt that it was–he had the will in his hands to prove it–then he had to find a wife.

Eleven months approximately before his time was up. Before his uncle made the trip across the Atlantic and took back what was rightfully Hugo's. His birthright.

Well, he wouldn't have it. He would adhere to the clause, but he would enjoy his final year as an unmarried gentleman as well. There was nothing he disliked more than being told by his father what to do. That his sire had managed this from beyond the grave was not something he'd thought the old curmudgeon capable of, but alas, he was wrong.

He swore. Eleven months and then, and only then would he find a willing heiress wanting a marriage of convenience, and be done with it.

In all the past Seasons he'd failed to find anyone who inspired him with anything other than with lust, so, in the next season, he would marry a biddable heiress to secure his properties. A perfectly convenient plan if ever he had one.

Under no circumstances was he willing to lose his lands, have to lease out his estates, and live off meager funds for the rest of his life. His name would be ruined; he'd be a lord pitied by everyone. The Wakelys had never had to ask for money, and he would not be the first one to do so. He shuddered. Oh no, that would never do.

Heiress hunting he would go. Well, in eleven months in any case.

ONE

Ten months later. Garden party, London

"It says right here in Pride and Prejudice that a gentleman in possession of a large fortune must be in want of a wife." Lizzie Doherty slapped the book shut and noticed her cousin by marriage, the Countess of Leighton, making an amused study of her. "What are the odds my very sentiments are confirmed in these novels. What do you say, Kat?"

Katherine laughed, shaking her head. "Lizzie, that unfortunately is not always true, and then when it is, the man usually makes the catastrophic mistake of marrying someone they don't care about, or even like for that matter. And you're not a man, you're a woman in possession of a large fortune, if not known within society, and so it's you who is looking for a husband."

Lizzie stared down at Pride and Prejudice, thinking over her cousin's words, which unfortunately her last Season in town had proved correct. Despite her connections, no one had offered for her hand, nor suggested they might, in all the balls she attended. It had even started to frustrate her, and she wasn't normally the type to become annoyed at other people's decisions or actions. But to be a pariah for an unknown reason seemed peculiar. And now, she'd had enough of it.

Lizzie came from a family with great connections, even if they were on the poor side of the Upper Ten Thousand. Her own situation was improved when her cousin Hamish, Earl Leighton, bestowed on her a large dowry some six years ago, which had only grown in value over that time due to his investments, or so he'd told her. She was set to be gifted close to seventy thousand pounds upon her marriage, or her twenty-fifth birthday. A tidy sum any future husband would be happy to receive. If one would only ask her.

Lizzie smiled, giving thanks every day for her mother's decision to send her to town all those years ago to have her Season with Lord Leighton's mother, even if she wasn't the most pleasant woman to be about.

She sighed as her mother came to join them, flicking her fan shut with a snap. "Oh, for heaven's sake, Lizzie, stop sitting here with Lady Leighton and go and stand out on the lawn with the young ladies your own age. You're the epitome of a wallflower at this very moment."

Lord Leighton had thought it best that they keep the fact Lizzie was now an heiress from both their mothers, due to their inability to keep secrets. The last thing they wanted to do was make her susceptible to fortune hunters. And so, at picnics such as the one they were at today, Lizzie had to tolerate her mother's chastisement over her failure to catch a husband. But it was harder than one thought, especially when all the men believed you were poor.

"I see your friend Sally has arrived, Lizzie. You had better go say hello," Katherine said, winking at her.

"I shall, thank you," she said, standing and starting toward her friend. She took in the guests at Lord and Lady Hart's picnic. She had found that a lot of the gentlemen only wanted a rich wife, or worse, were just carousing and seeing if any delectable widows were up for a naughty jaunt in their carriages. Of course, Lizzie wasn't supposed to know what was happening behind the closed doors of the London *ton*, but one would be a simpleton indeed if they thought all those who paid attendance on them, made house calls, and had the best intentions outwardly, were always angels.

A distinct whisper tittered through the guests and Lizzie turned to see Lord Hugo Blythe, Viscount Wakely, join the picnic, bowing to the hosts before walking toward the Duke and Duchess of Athelby.

Lizzie took the opportunity to watch him, not unlike so many other women at this very moment. But when one was faced with the fine, athletic form of Lord Wakely, one ought to stop and admire the view.

His lordship oozed the forbidden deliciousness that she shouldn't know anything about. But if one listened carefully enough at balls and parties, you could always pick up tidbits of information about what society was up to. Who was having an affair with whom, who was a terrible lover or had vices at both table and horses. The things Lizzie had heard her first Season in town, many years ago now, would've been enough to make her mother have a turn of the vapours had she disclosed them.

Now, six years later, she was a well-known wallflower, or at least a debutante too long in the tooth to be considered for marriage. Not that it mattered, due to the sizable dowry she would be gifted either upon her marriage or on her twenty-fifth birthday. And since she was closer to being five and twenty than she was to marriage, the allure of not marrying at all had taken hold in her mind and wouldn't dislodge. There were worse things in life than being unmarried, such as marrying the wrong kind of man, or having a loveless marriage. Marrying a man who sought the comfort of others, even after their marriage vows were spoken. She would rather remain single and become a spinster than make such an unchangeable, catastrophic mistake.

Lord Wakely grinned devilishly toward a group of giggling debutantes, but despite his teasing and mirth, not once did he falter in his gentlemanly behaviour. And yet, Lizzie wondered what was really going on behind his dark, stormy blue eyes. What did he really think about being one of London's most sought-after bachelors? Did he enjoy the attention or merely tolerate it? After all, his lordship even had the ability to make Lizzie's stomach flutter. Her heart pumped faster whenever their gazes clashed.

It was a reaction she'd never experienced with anyone else, in all her years dancing in the ballrooms of London. She'd known him for some years now, her cousin having introduced them during her second Season. Although she couldn't tell what effect she'd had on him, if any, Lizzie had lost her breath a little that day they'd met and never really got it back.

He seemed to have been born with the most luscious dark hair she'd ever seen, His skin had a beautiful olive tone to it, not pasty white like so many English gentlemen. She took a sip of her champagne, having forgotten to go to her friend, and instead remained standing by the cake table watching him. She pursed her lips, wondering if he had any Spanish blood in the family, with a jawline that looked like it could cut glass, not to mention his perfectly proportioned nose.

One day someone would snatch him up, make him fall desperately in love with them, and how lucky would that lady be. To wake up each morning next to such a man would be heavenly indeed.

Her friend Sally spotted her and waved. Putting Lord Wakely out of her mind, Lizzie joined her just as the woman Sally was speaking to, Lady Jersey, bade her good day.

Lizzie kissed Sally on the cheek and accepted a fresh glass of champagne from a passing footman. "I so wish Mama would stop making me attend these types of events where we're paraded like cattle at Tattersalls. I'm getting too old to worry about men and marriage, and my mother has a tendency to throw every rich youth at my head, even when it's quite obvious I'm too old for them and that they're absolutely in no way interested in me."

Sally chuckled, her eyes twinkling in mirth. "You are not too old. Why, for a man, you're not even considered in your prime. You debuted so young, only seventeen, it is no wonder you're sick of all these games and courtship dances."

Lizzie nodded, agreeing with everything Sally said. Her friend always spoke the truth and without exaggeration. She was truly the best person Lizzie knew, other than her cousin Hamish. "You are right of course. And I will admit the Season is getting awfully stale. I long for adventure. I will tell you this Sally, because I know you're my friend and as silent as the grave, but if I could, I'd purchase a home of my own, move away from Mama, and procure a cat. Or better yet, lots of cats. I will be well satisfied once all of those three things are complete."

Sally shook her head, smiling. "I don't believe you for a

second. I know very well there is a certain gentleman who'd change your spinster ideals in a trice should he court you. What a pity he's so elusive, even though quite polite to us young, inexperienced females. Although I did hear a whisper that he's on the hunt for a wife. Perhaps you may be in the running..."

Lizzie laughed, as understanding dawned. She looked around the gardens and found him without trouble, and inwardly sighed at how darling he was in every way. "How handsome he is. Do you think he knows that every woman in London is in love with him? I wonder if he has any Spanish blood in him. He has the most beautiful olive-toned skin I've ever seen."

"Why, yes, I think you're right. From memory I do believe his grandmother was from Portugal. Maybe that's where he inherited his dark good looks." Her friend studied him a moment before she said, "Lord Wakely could pass for a pirate—rugged, sun-touched and terribly naughty, from what the gossip rags state." She grinned, taking a sip of her drink.

"His outwardly features are to be praised, but he is good at heart too. Why, last year he made a sizable donation to the London Relief Society that the Duchess of Athelby and Marchioness of Aaron run. And he always dances with debutantes new to town, and gives them a good start to their Season. He is never unkind. In fact, I've never heard a bad word about him, not regarding his manners or temperament. What a shame there is chatter that he's after Miss Edwina Fox." Just the mention of this debutante made Lizzie's teeth ache. "She debuted this year and is the talk of the *ton* since her uncle is related to the Duke of Athelby. Well-connected and rich...exactly what all young gentleman seek in a wife, is it not?"

"Your final words dripped with sarcasm, Lizzie. Perhaps you should be less cutting when we're in company," Sally suggested. "Are you looking forward to Lady Remmnick's house party? We're leaving early tomorrow morning–father wishes to arrive well before the afternoon. With everyone who's invited, I doubt there will be many left in town."

Lizzie couldn't wait to return to the country, the fresh air, and the horse riding she would be able to do more often. "I am looking forward to it, and I cannot thank your mama enough for allowing me to go under her chaperonage. Although I will arrive the day after tomorrow with my maid. Mama is going home to Bellview Manor and I'll travel onto the Remmnicks' from there."

Sally clasped her arm, walking them about the fringes of the lawn. "I'm so excited to attend. Arthur will be there. Do you think he'll finally ask me to marry him if he can manage to drag me away from Mama for one moment?"

Marquess Mongrove–or Arthur to Sally and Lizzie, since they'd known him since childhood–was the newly appointed Marquess and finally able to decide for himself what his future would be. Not his mother, which Lizzie could sympathize with since she too had an overbearing parent. He'd been a pleasant child and had grown into a lovely gentleman that suited Sally and her honest and obliging temperament. A perfect match for her friend in all ways.

"I'm sure he will. In fact, look at him now pining for you over there under the elm tree. How sad he looks that he hasn't got his love beside him, hanging off his every word and worshipping the ground he stands upon."

Sally slapped her arm. "Stop your teasing." She smiled. "He is lovely though, I must agree, and should he ask me to be his wife, I will say yes immediately and request a very hasty marriage. I'm ready for my life as a wife and mother to start. I see no point in waiting before we say our vows, if you understand my meaning."

Lizzie smiled at the light blush that stole across her friend's cheeks. "You'll make a beautiful bride and a perfect, loving wife. Lord Mongrove will be lucky to have you."

"Thank you, dearest." Sally threw his lordship a small wave, delighting when he waved back in return. "I simply cannot wait another day, and so I suppose this house party has come at a perfect time. We each need a little diversion from life's trials."

Lizzie couldn't agree more.

"Not to mention," Sally continued, turning her attention back to her, "we'll be away from town and staying under one roof. What fun we will have. And even though my head is already turned, it does not mean you cannot find someone to love."

"There is only one gentleman I want, and he doesn't even know that I exist. I'm simply the cousin of one of his closest friends, unremarkable and forgettable at best. And as I've stated before, I'll not marry anyone simply to procure children and do my duty. Whomever I marry, it will be for love. Such a deep, heart-wrenching, all-consuming love that it will simply drive away all my dreams of my own home, vacant of parents and filled with cats."

"I like this plan. It suits you well, and you know I want nothing but the very best for you," Sally declared, her tone serious.

"Do you know if Lord Wakely is attending the Remmnicks' house party?" Lizzie asked, trying but failing desperately to hide the hope that was in her tone. Oh dear, she really was desperate and pining for the man. If only she could curb her enthusiasm toward him and see other gentlemen for their worth. When there were some, of course.

Sally grimaced and Lizzie had her answer before her friend uttered a word. "Unfortunately, he's not attending, although I was told he will be in the county attending another event. Not far from the Remmnicks' estate, in fact."

Lizzie bit her lip and wondered what this other event was, and who was attending. The social set his lordship was part of were the elite of society. Only gentlemen of extreme wealth and with very few cares in the world were allowed entry. Gentlemen who loved the frivolities of societal living, and the luxurious lifestyle and loose women that their status afforded them. No rules and no wives allowed.

It was not for the faint of heart, and certainly nothing like Lizzie could ever imagine for herself had she been a man and able to join such an association. Not that she was supposed to know any of these things, but some gossip was too juicy to ignore. "I will not deny that I'm somewhat disappointed by that news, but then he doesn't even know that I exist, so what does it matter which event he attends?"

Sally clasped her arm and cuddled her a little to her side. "Do not be downcast, dearest. There is a gentleman out there with your name written on him. And you shall marry him and love him wildly when you find him."

Lizzie laughed, not even able to imagine such a possibility, but wishing it nonetheless. If only to get away from her mama, who could at times be terribly stifling, sooner than her twenty-fifth birthday. "Only time will tell, I suppose."

Not that she would tell Sally, but Lizzie was content

waiting for her endowment from Hamish, because it was far more likely than being noticed by the viscount. If he had any interest in her at all, he would have made his intentions clear years ago.

"It will tell, my dear, and when it does, it'll be a great story to hear."

CHAPTER

TWO

Kent — two days later

T he carriage rocked alarmingly, and Lizzie clasped a strap beside the window with two hands to stop herself from tumbling to the floor. Her maid let out a squeak when once more the carriage slipped on the muddy track, sending them to sway about like leaves in the wind.

"Oh, Miss Lizzie, this is terrible. If we do not arrive soon I fear we'll never make it."

It was a fear Lizzie herself had had multiple times already since they set off from her family's estate early that morning. The weather from the south had come in so fast that by the time they'd left the last inn where they'd changed horses it was too late to go back.

A howling sound whirred through the door and Lizzie shivered. "I'm sure the storm will pass soon. Do not worry, Mary. We'll be there shortly, I promise."

Tears sprang in her maid's eyes and Lizzie looked

outside. Night was falling fast and still no sign of lights could be seen, no beacon of safety in this terrible storm.

The carriage rocked to a halt, then dipped as the driver jumped down. Lizzie opened the door and it was wrenched open by the howling wind, hitting the side of the carriage with such force the window smashed onto the carriage seat. Her maid screamed, and she cursed.

"Miss Lizzie, we're at a crossroads, and the storm's blown over the sign showing the direction of Lady Remmnick's estate," her driver yelled, the sheeting rain making it hard to hear what anyone was saying.

She shivered, squinting as the rain pelted against her face. "Go left and we'll hope for the best."

"Right ye are," he said, shutting the door and leaving them alone once more.

Lizzie reached under the carriage seat and pulled out a blanket, handing it to her maid. "Push the glass away with this and we'll try to block the window a little."

Her maid did as she bade, and with a little trouble they managed to keep some of the weather from intruding into the vehicle. Not very successfully though, and by the time the carriage did arrive at the estate, both Lizzie and Mary were drenched and shivering with cold.

A footman ran from inside the well-lit home, a most welcome haven after their ordeal.

Lizzie stepped down and ran indoors along with her maid. Inside, a woman she'd never met before strode toward them, with a calm assurance and grace that was the opposite of how Lizzie looked and felt at that exact moment. In fact, she was pretty sure she was leaving a terrible wet puddle on the mosaic tiled floor.

"Welcome, you've arrived just in time."

Lizzie dipped into a curtsy, wondering where Lady

Remmnick was as this woman certainly wasn't her lady-ship. A servant walked past with a tray of champagne, and through an ajar door Lizzie spotted guests with masks, even though the lady before her didn't have one herself. "Thank you so much for inviting me, but I must apologize for my tardy arrival. The weather outside is atrocious and we almost lost our way."

"You're right on time. If you follow me upstairs, I'll show you to your room where you can change."

"Thank you," Lizzie said, looking about and taking in the home. The silence was deafening, and she frowned. Normally house parties were lively, with people milling about all over the place. The guests in the adjacent room were oddly quiet. "I'm Miss Lizzie Doherty by the way, and you are? I suspect Lady Remmnick is busy with the guests who are already here."

The woman stopped, placing a finger against her lips and shaking her head in silence. "No one has names here. Not for the next three days at least, my dear."

Lizzie stopped on the staircase's top step, her maid's furrowed brow reflecting her own thoughts. "May I enquire as to whose estate this is?"

The lady laughed, a sultry sound that caused unease to coil through her blood. "That's a secret too, although I'm sure you're only teasing. You received an invite after all. You must have, to be here. The location is secret." The woman paused, turning to face her. Lizzie met her inspection and wondered if she looked as pathetic as she felt standing before this golden goddess. "You did receive an invite, yes?"

"I did, yes, but—"

"Well then, you may follow me and join the party once you've cleaned yourself up. We have recently had running water installed upstairs in every room, so you may have a bath if you wish. The gowns that are suitable for wear are in your armoire, and tonight's color requirement is green, so please use a gown that's appropriate. Your maid will find an appropriate mask in the tallboy."

Lizzie followed without saying a word, her mind a whirr of thoughts. Was this a new event Lady Remmnick had introduced at her house party? The approach was indeed intriguing. Lizzie would go along for now, but when she found Sally she would enquire about the details.

A familiar laugh sounded, and she looked over the balustrade and spotted Lord Wakely coming out of one of the rooms downstairs. His stride and voice were as familiar as Lizzie's own, so she would've known him anywhere, even if right now he had a black mask covering half his face. He was not supposed to be at Lady Remmnick's house party.

Clarity bloomed into Lizzie's mind as it dawned upon her that it was she and not he who was at the wrong house party.

She bit her lip, butterflies fluttering in her belly at the thought of him being here. This must be the house party that her friend Sally had been talking about. The one that was coveted by anyone who was anyone within the *ton*. And invite only.

What was it that everyone got up to here that was so secretive?

"This is your room, my dear."

With a flourish, the woman showed Lizzie into her bedchamber situated at the end of a long corridor. A frisson of excitement ran through her that she was actually here. Even if she wasn't supposed to be. How fortuitous that the current evening's activity was a masquerade.

Lizzie walked into the room and marvelled at the beautiful furniture and decorations throughout. A large bed with a canopy rested before the windows. She'd never seen such a layout before, but didn't mind it in the least. It looked delightful, in fact. There was a large tub for bathing, along with a wash basin and bowl. Two high-backed chairs sat before the fire, with deep green covering that suited the dark wooden floor and the green coverlet on the bed. It wasn't the least feminine, nor overly masculine either. In fact, it was just a perfectly lovely, welcoming room.

"This is quite acceptable. Thank you," Lizzie said, setting down her bonnet on the ladies writing desk.

"I'll have one of my own maids sent up to show your girl what you should wear and when. I will see you in an hour downstairs for dinner."

Lizzie nodded, trying dreadfully hard not to show her nerves at what she was about to embark on. At any time she could be caught and sent home, ruined beyond repair because she had no chaperone present.

As soon as the door closed behind the mysterious woman, Mary turned toward her, her eyes as round as the moon. "Miss Lizzie, ye can't stay here. This house, these guests...well, did ye see the gentleman that was about downstairs? He had a mask on, covering himself for some reason. I have a feeling this party is not like the ones you are used to."

Lizzie looked out the window and a black, stormy night greeted her. Should this party be what she assumed it to be, one of ill repute and debauchery, there was little she could do about it now. She was here whether she wanted to be or not, and there was no way they could leave for the Remmnicks' house party in this weather.

The gale rattled the window as if in agreement and Lizzie pulled the heavy velvet drapes closed to keep it at bay. But she also couldn't help but thank providence that she had arrived on this doorstep instead of Lady Remmnick's. For years there had been rumors–tales of debauchery regarding the parties Lord Wakely attended. Now she had a chance to see for herself what was fiction and what was truth.

"I will bathe and change into what they wish me to wear, put on my mask, and at the first opportunity tomorrow we shall leave. No one will guess who we are if you stay here in the adjacent room, and I'll keep my identity secret. Something I'm guessing they wish us to do, since we're not to use any names at all or show our faces."

"Well, ye can't go about the house as no one. What name shall you use if you're asked?"

Good question. Lizzie frowned. She had always liked Eve as a name, and it would do should she have to come up with something. "If anyone asks, call me Mrs. Eve Jacobs, a widow from Cumbria. That's far enough away that no one would've ever heard of me."

"And your husband died how?"

A light knock sounded on the door and her maid bid another young woman welcome. The young lady showed Mary how to pour the bath and where the linen was kept before laying out Lizzie's dress for the evening and showing Mary where the masks were kept.

Once they were alone again, and Lizzie was undressing for the bath, she said, "A tumor in his belly is what killed my husband. Not that I expect anyone to ask, or that servants would be enquiring about me, but just in case. I'm sure they've seen these sorts of events before, where questions are frowned upon."

"I will do as ye ask, Miss Lizzie. I promise," Mary said, turning off the tap.

The hot water of the hipbath was a welcoming delight after the cold journey they had endured. She sent Mary away and shut her eyes. Images of Lord Wakely filled her mind. His mask made him look forbidden, dangerous, and her nipples puckered in response. She ran the soap over her body, imagining his lordship's hands instead, and a heavy longing ached between her legs. For so long she'd wanted to throw herself at his head and see if he'd have any response to her, such as the visceral response she'd always had with him.

His satin knee breeches and gleaming hessians had accentuated his athletic form. He was certainly not a man who lay about. Much too perfectly shaped for that. As for his coat and perfectly tied cravat, and the pieces of his hair hanging about his mask, she could only agree that what Sally said about him resembling a pirate really did ring true. Maybe he'd plunder her.

She chuckled at her own unladylike imaginings and washed away the soap. In all seriousness, she really ought to take into account what her being here could mean for her future. Her cousin may have gifted her an endowment, but it didn't come without certain obligations that had to be met. Hamish had stipulated that he would speak to whomever Lizzie wished for as a husband, and if he found him genuine, and in love with Lizzie, he would give his blessing on the marriage, and thus pave the way for her to receive her fortune. Should Hamish not come to this conclusion upon meeting her intended, he would not allow the marriage to proceed.

To maintain her reputation, it was essential that no one found out she was here. And if she did approach Lord Wakely, would he have any interest in her? Or would he send her away? Lizzie sighed, touching her lips and wondering if his kiss would be as sweet and all-consuming as she imagined it to be. He was a renowned rake, so he would certainly know what to do...

She threw the soap away, her mind made up. She would go downstairs disguised, and see how the night progressed. The storm made it impossible to leave, but that did not mean she had to spend the night enclosed within her chambers. If Lord Wakely happened to take a liking to her masked self, she would enjoy a stolen kiss or two but nothing else. Never would she put her future in jeopardy. Not when she was so close to having her hands upon her fortune, all for herself and without anyone else lording it over her for the rest of her life.

If she could not find a husband who loved her, she would love all that her fortune could give her instead.

CHAPTER

THREE

Hugo stood at the piano, listening as their hostess Lady X, as she liked to be known, even though all those in attendance knew she was really Lady Xenia Campbell, a widow whose husband had died during a carriage race. She had chosen a lovely sedate piece of music from Mozart to the gathered throng that did not impinge on or distract from what the guests were discussing. A lover of music, Hugo leaned over the pianoforte and surveyed the room and all the guests who had arrived over the last day.

All of them were up to mischief and wanting to escape the confines of London Society and what was expected of them. All of them wanted to be here to partake in the pleasures of the flesh without censure or guilt. He had attended quite a few of these events over the years, and sometimes even partook in the games that were afoot, but alas this would be his last. After his father's last decree in his will, Hugo had only until July twenty-third to procure a wife, or he'd be without funds to continue the life to which he was accustomed.

His initial reaction to being told what to do had been rebellion, and he'd done everything he could not to look for a wife. But of late he'd felt restless, disillusioned with the games and intrigues within the *ton*. He'd decided that Miss Edwina Fox, an untitled gentleman's daughter with a fortune that would suit the terms of his father's will, would suit his pocket very well. She was honest, not a silly young woman, maybe a little cold and aloof, but marriage to her might be tolerable enough. He did not love her, but he certainly liked her very much. And with the time constraints he was now under, she would have to do. There was little time left to look for another suitable bride.

The parlor door opened, and he wrenched himself upright, almost spilling his whisky as he did so. What the devil was Lizzie Doherty doing here?

His gaze devoured her like a man starved of food. Her dark emerald gown brought out her perfect cream skin and made her fiery auburn hair positively shine. Not to mention her breasts were amply advertised. He shut his mouth with a snap. Never had he seen her dressed so provocatively, presenting herself for the taking. She didn't move, simply took in the room, and the breath in his lungs froze while his blood pumped hot in his veins.

She was magnificent. A small smile tweaked his lips. How could he not admire her being so bold, so brave, when she had one of the strictest mothers in all England?

Hugo took in the room's reaction and frowned, not liking the fact that all the gentleman present were admiring her, some with a hunger that matched his own.

He'd not let any of them touch one hair on her body. She was his, and his alone. If anyone was going to pluck her innocence it would be him.

He took a calming breath, reeling himself back to real-

24

ity. What was he thinking? He could not touch her either. To even imagine taking her to bed was such a breach of trust that he'd never be able to re-establish the friendship between himself and Lord Leighton. He fisted his hands, fighting his body that had hardened at the sight of her, even knowing who she was.

Thank the lord for the masks they wore, well-made ones that ensured no one's identity was absolutely obvious. Even if most of the guests knew by now who everyone was, it was not always the case, as it seemed right now with Lizzie. Yes, he'd picked her out, but one was wont to do such a thing when one often appreciated the lithe, delicate, and yet bountifully gifted Lizzie in person.

With a strength Hugo had always known she possessed, Lizzie steeled her back, raised her chin, and met the ogling guests head on.

Lord Finley sauntered up to her, and Hugo ground his teeth. The gentleman had hands as slimy as an eel's skin and was a regular at these parties. Always willing to shove his cock into anything agreeable.

"Friend of yours, sir?"

Hugo turned to his hostess and shook his head. The last person he would tell was Lady X. She was as meddling as his father at times, and he didn't need any more people interfering in his life.

Lady X chuckled as she continued to play. "Miss Lizzie Doherty, I believe. Not that I'm going to tell anyone here, mind you. But I greeted her late this afternoon when she arrived. I've had it from my steward that her carriage was turned about in this afternoon's storm and they arrived here instead of Lady Remmnick's house party three miles away. If she keeps her identify a secret, no harm shall come of her."

So that was how she came to be here. He didn't think Lizzie was into the kind of lifestyle most of the people present enjoyed. Not unless she was living in a world he knew nothing of. "You should've told her to stay in her room and not come out. You know what goes on at these types of parties. Hell, she's a lovely sweetmeat just ripe for the eating."

"And would you like to eat her, my lord?" His hostess grinned up at him, devilment in her gaze. "Something tells me you would."

Hugo wouldn't deny the charge, nor would he answer such a question. Did he wish to eat the delectable little Lizzie? Hell yes, he did...had for a very long time. Over the months that they had been thrown together due to their mutual friendships, and her relationship to the Earl and Countess of Leighton, he'd become quite fond of her. Had she not been a poor relative of the Earl, Hugo would've courted her instead of Miss Fox. He certainly liked her more than anyone he'd ever previously met, and found she brought forth in him a hunger he'd not known before with any other woman.

Certainly, he was too fond to allow her to lose herself to the pretty talk and false promises that the current Lord Finley was no doubt whispering in her ear.

"Do not tell anyone of her being here. I will make certain she returns to Lady Remmnick's house party on the morrow."

Lady X nodded. "I think that would be best."

Hugo strolled about the room, keeping his attention sporadically fixed on Lizzie. How beautiful she looked tonight in her green, revealing empire cut gown. The dress appeared to be a size too small, and her breasts, which had always been generous, filled the top of the garment more than they should. It fell about her slender frame, her silver slippered shoes peeking out from beneath the hem.

Without being obvious, he made his way to Lizzie's side, although by the time he arrived his patience had waned, just as his temper had spiked at the attention the little minx was getting from those who ought to know better. What was worse was that Hugo knew that even if some of the gentlemen who courted her now were aware of who she was, it would make not one ounce of difference. They would still wish to seduce her, have and enjoy all that she could give them, and walk away leaving her to fend for herself.

He bowed, taking her gloved hand and kissing it in welcome. "I do not believe we've been introduced." Lord Finlay glared at his interruption, but didn't comment, simply stood by, silent.

Her eyes widened, and his interest spiked. Did she know who he was? Would she run away or stay if she did? Lizzie dipped into a perfect curtsy, her rouge-covered lips lifting into a grin. Desire rushed through his veins and without doubt Hugo confirmed his suspicions. He wanted her. In his bed. His and only his. Which, he reminded himself, he couldn't do. He wasn't able to marry a woman with no dowry. Maybe she'd be open to a stolen kiss before he sent her home... It was worth a thought.

"My lord," she said, not an ounce of fear in her voice.

"My lady," he said, although he knew she held no title to speak of. At these parties it had been long agreed that no names should be spoken, and that everyone was a lord and lady in this environment, even if they acted less than the ideal their name would normally be associated with.

"You're new to our gathering. Are you enjoying the night so far?"

She smiled, and there was no doubt left in his mind as to who stood before him. "I am, yes. It's been quite pleasant so far."

Lord Benedict approached and bowed over her hand, placing a lingering kiss on her wrist. "And mayhap the night will end pleasurably for you too, my lady...should you choose me, that is."

The need to pummel Lord Benedict into dirt on the Aubusson rug was almost too much to resist. But she was new to these events and so every gentleman, and some ladies, would want to experience her mystery. Lizzie's cheeks flushed bright red and Hugo took her arm, steering her away from the party. "Some wine, perhaps," he said, turning their backs on the confounded lord.

"Thank you. I fear I'm not used to such...entertainments."

"So, you've never attended one of these parties before? I thought you were new. I would've remembered you." He was flirting, and her coquettish smile made him want to tease her even more, if only to see more of the same.

"No, never." She took the glass of wine he offered and, to his amusement, downed it almost immediately.

"Refreshing?"

She laughed, placing her glass on the tray of a passing footman before taking another. "In need of fortifying, more like."

Hugo chuckled and nodded in agreement. If the elixir of drink helped her relax in the environment she now found herself, who was he to naysay her? He would however remain by her side and ensure that no harm came to her reputation, and no rake that now graced the parlor went within a foot of her person. Unless it was him of course.

It was the least he could do, being a family friend. Or so he kept telling himself.

——————

SOME HOURS LATER—DELIGHTFUL, EXCITING HOURS AT THAT—LIZZIE strolled toward her room, her body very aware of the tall, masculine frame walking beside her. Hugo stood back as she came to her door, and Lizzie wished the night wouldn't end. What would he do if she were to proposition him? Turn her away, or take her in his arms?

She licked her lips at the thought of being held by him as she wished. After all the months that she had lusted after this gentleman, to have him before her, quite alone and without the worry of being caught since this party was for the very purpose of being naughty, was a temptation she wanted to explore.

She reached out and touched the lapels of his coat. Lord Wakely stilled under her palm. Having watched the other ladies tonight waltz a dance of seduction with their chosen gentlemen, Lizzie had picked up on a couple of ideas. She leaned forward, placing her body scandalously close to his, and his eyes darkened in hunger.

The entire evening he'd stayed by her side, ensuring her every comfort was met, so would he now ensure her every desire was as well? Surely that meant she was about to be kissed. Her first kiss, and with a man she'd long admired as well as desired. Not that she was willing to throw her maid-enhead out the window, but a kiss couldn't hurt.

"I hope you enjoyed your first night?" he asked, leaning against the door's threshold, his cravat untied and hanging loose about his neck. She itched to rip it off and slide her hands over his chest, not just his lapels, and feel the muscles respond to her touch.

"I did, thank you. It has been quite entertaining and eye opening as well." Like when she had seen the Countess of Eden, whose mask had slipped during a passionate kiss with one of the first gentlemen who'd bowed before her upon arrival in the parlor. They had all but bundled each other out of the room and not returned. Lizzie had little doubt as to what the couple were up to at this very moment. Heat bloomed on her cheeks and she bit her lip, thanking providence that his lordship couldn't read minds.

"That tends to be the case at these parties." He closed the space even further between them, so that her breasts were brushing his chest and coiling heat to her core. He kissed her cheek and her knees wobbled. Without thought she leaned into the embrace, closing her eyes as the smell of sandalwood intoxicated her senses. Lord Wakely paused a moment, his breath whispering foreign words against her neck.

"Do you attend these parties often, my lord?" The question came out breathless and she cursed knowing he would be aware of what his nearness did to her. Made her want things no respectable woman would dare think of. Made her yearn for a man's touch over that of respectability or propriety. She fisted his lapels in her hands, holding him close.

"This is my last." He kissed the lobe of her ear and she shivered.

"Why is that?" He kissed her ear again and she bit back a moan. Golly he made her ache, made her want so much.

Her attention snapped to his lips. His hand clasped her nape, his fingers tangling into her hair. This was it. Right here and now, Lord Wakely was going to kiss her. Show her everything she'd been missing all these years. Her body shook with expectation and she leaned up on tiptoe to better meet his height.

He pulled back, severing their nearness, and she stumbled a little before righting herself. He watched her a moment, a muscle working in his jaw. "That, my dear, is a conversation best had on another day." He bowed. "I will be across the hall should you need any assistance."

Lizzie watched his lordship run away from her as if she had the pox, his door closing with more force than was necessary. She slumped against the door frame, frowning. Why had he run away like that? These parties were supposed to end with seduction and pleasure, or at the very least a passionate kiss that would make her toes curl in her slippers. Unless he knew who she was and wouldn't touch her because of her cousin Lord Leighton, one of his best friends?

If he did suspect who she was, it meant that his attendance on her this evening had been wholly to ensure she remained safe and not assaulted by the other gentlemen present. Disappointment stabbed her. How mortifying if that were true. And she'd thrown herself at his head like a desperate ninny. Her cheeks burned, and tears blurred her vision.

Mary was waiting for her when she came into her room, and with her maid's help, Lizzie was soon in bed, reliving the feel of his lips on her cheek, and then again on her earlobe. A disturbing little thrum thumped between her legs at the memory and she rolled over, squeezing her thighs together to soothe the need that coursed through her.

How could he bring forth such a reaction within her if she meant nothing to him? Could men have reactions to women in such a way? Did it even matter who warmed their bed, just so long as someone did? If he was never interested in kissing her in the first place, why had he kissed her neck? It made no sense.

Could men be so fickle?

The sound of the pounding rain on the window lulled her for a time, but it did little to soothe her disappointed hopes. When he'd sought her out early in the evening she'd felt such anticipation that the night would end in a kiss. That he would find her interesting and charming. She could only conclude that he knew who she was and was being a gentleman, a good friend to her cousin. The embrace before bidding her goodnight had been a slip in his armor and nothing else. He might even have done it to try to scare her off, tell her without words that this party was not for her and she shouldn't be here.

For if there was one thing she knew for sure about Lord Wakely, it was that he took what he wanted. That he didn't take her was all she needed to know.

Just like her life in London, here at Lady X's house party, she was undesirable. A wallflower destined for the spinster shelf. Well, at least she'd have her cats for company, and bucketloads of money. It was better than nothing.

FOUR

Lizzie rolled over in her bed and stared at the ceiling of her room. Images of men and women in very compromising positions looked down at her, their smiles and gazes of satisfaction mocking her and her inability to seduce the man she wanted. Had wanted for an age.

Here she was, at the most sought-after party of the Season, and she'd failed to gain a kiss from a man who was famous in the *ton* for seduction. She looked at the discarded mask she'd worn the night before. No one should've recognized her wearing it, but Lord Wakely wasn't everyone.

Did he know who she was? And if so, even though he hadn't kissed her, why didn't he send her packing the moment he realized who graced the scandalous house party? For all his rakehell ways, as a gentleman he would see such a task as only right and honorable.

But he had not. In fact, he'd flirted with her for most of the night. His attentions prior to dinner were telling, as were his hot stares throughout the meal, not to mention that kiss before saying goodnight. Well, a chaste peck against her cheek, her ear, her neck...

She sighed, looking at the curtains still drawn against the morning sun. Getting up, she walked over to them and pulled one back, taking in the landscape before her. This side of the home sported a lawned area that flowed like a green sea into the oak forest a little way away. From here she could just make out the roof of a summer house hidden amongst the woodland. There were many leaves and small sticks lying on the ground from the previous night's storm, and she watched for a moment as a gardener tried to clear away as much as he could.

Sensing movement on the terrace below, she looked down and watched as the very gentleman who haunted her dreams smoked a cheroot while leaning casually against the terrace balustrade. From here she could make very little out of his features, and yet his height and stature gave him away.

He stood outdoors, covered only by a thin white shirt that did nothing to hide his muscular form, which flexed beneath the shirt with the smallest amount of movement. Lizzie sighed, admiring his muscled thighs that today were encased in tan, skin-tight breeches. Not for the first time she was jealous of whoever ended up marrying him.

He walked along the terrace, looking out on the grounds as well, and she realized he wore no boots. She'd never seen a man's feet before, and seeing Lord Wakely's only left her eager to see more of him in a similarly naked way.

She ran her finger along the pane of glass. What a shame it was that men like Lord Wakely were never interested in the meek, mild debutantes who graced Almack's with their parents in hand. Something she was still unfortunately doing, since her mother wasn't privy to her endowment. She only had two more years and the money her cousin had bestowed upon her would be hers, marriage no longer a necessity. Her mother could be told then, when she no longer had any say in her life. Until then, Lizzie was happy to behave, and do as she was told.

Men like Lord Wakely enjoyed women, married or otherwise, such as the ones at this house party. They only wanted their wives to grace ballrooms with elegance and accomplishment that would do their names proud, but never to love and be besotted by them. Unless they were cut from a different cloth, like her cousin Lord Leighton, the Duke of Athelby, or the Marquess of Aaron, who were the exceptions to that rule.

A longing to know what it was exactly that went on between husband and wife assailed Lizzie, and with it an urge to stomp her foot. Last evening she should have pressed him for more, taken what she wanted and be damned the consequence.

She should've shoved her fears aside and kissed him, not concerned herself with what he would say and do. Then, if he had sent her home without touching her, without bestowing her first kiss, well, it wouldn't have been without trying. In any case his rejection of her hurt, but at least if she had been brave she would've had a kiss, chaste as it might be, before she was bade goodnight.

Now, she seemed to have missed her chance. If the rumors were true, he was courting Miss Fox—a woman with ducal titles in her blood, who would bring to marriage numerous estates, and money. Lots of it. Did he care for that woman? Was that why he pulled away? The *ton* whispered that the union would only be a marriage of convenience, but maybe it wasn't. The thought depressed her. She didn't want Lord Wakely to want anyone else.

The memory of his kiss against her neck hinted that the union was indeed one of convenience, which left her wondering why he wanted Miss Fox as his wife. Was his lordship looking to align himself with a woman of wealth? And if so, why? The Wakely family had always been affluent.

If his lordship was in need of funds, and by some miracle he did turn his attentions toward her, it was imperative that he not find out about her endowment. She could not stomach any man marrying her for money alone. Just as her cousin had stated all those years ago, if a man fell in love with her, as poor as he thought her, then he was the man worthy of her heart, and her fortune.

Lizzie sat down in the window nook. After seeing her cousin, the Earl Leighton, marry the love of his life, Kat, she could never settle for a marriage of convenience. No, she wanted so much more than that. Passion was what she desired. Passion and love. And without either of those emotions she would never marry at all, no matter what her mama had to say about it.

A knock at the door sounded and she jumped. A moment later, her maid entered with a breakfast tray laden with delicious food that made her stomach rumble.

Lizzie went about her morning routine, washing and breaking her fast before her maid helped her dress in a cream cotton morning gown with silk ribbons that trimmed the hem. Mary arranged her hair into a motif of curls, and as she pushed the last pin into position, the lady who had welcomed her the day before entered.

Her maid dipped into a curtsy and left to go to the adjacent room, giving them privacy. Lizzie stood. "Good morning, Lady X."

The woman didn't smile, but simply stood before her, hands clasped in front of her, a slight frown line marring her forehead. "I must apologize, Miss Doherty, for I have done you a most grievous injustice and one I shall remedy. I was a little hazy of mind after drinking champagne most of the afternoon yesterday, and I should never have played my little game and allowed you to join us downstairs last evening. Be assured that I'm doing all that I can to ensure your safe passage to Lady Remmnick's house party, which is the location you should have arrived at yesterday afternoon. I promise I shall do all that I can to keep your reputation intact after you leave."

Heat bloomed on Lizzie's cheeks and she cringed at being caught. "It is I who must apologize. I should have told you immediately that I was not whom you expected, and what had happened to us in the storm that ensured our arrival here. I hope I haven't put you out with my attendance. It was not purposely done."

Lady X came over and clasped Lizzie's hands. "You have not put me out in the slightest, but you have put your own reputation at extreme risk. My house parties are not like... well, let's just say, they are wicked. I'm sure you saw last night the happenings and goings on that occur. I thought it would be a lark to allow you one night, and then send you on your way today, but I was wrong. And now my keeping you here as a little distraction for myself may have put you in grave risk."

"Why so, my lady?" Lizzie asked. "We will simply ready the carriage and I shall be on my way. No harm in that."

Her ladyship sighed. "There is a stream that all vehicles in and out of the estate must pass through. It is flooded by the storm, terribly so in fact. Therefore, you are stranded here with us for at least three days. I am so sorry."

An array of emotions ran through Lizzie at her ladyship's words. Lord Wakely had walked away from their interlude. To have to face him again and not be able to leave and hide, to pretend she had never been here and ignore the fact she had offered herself up like a sweetmeat, was mortifying. Then again, another night under Lady X's roof could be her chance to change his mind... He had slipped a little and kissed her neck. Could she get him to do more than that if he knew she was willing?

They were to wear masks at all times, so her anonymity was secure. Even if he did suspect her, there was no way he could prove she was ever here, and she'd never admit it. Not to anyone.

Another night in his lordship's company could be a coup she'd not thought to have. "Will you sit, my lady? There is something I wish to tell you and you may need to be seated to hear it."

The woman raised her brow but did as Lizzie asked. She flattened her hands against her knees once seated on a nearby chair. "What is it you wish to tell me? I'm all ears, my dear."

Lizzie took a breath, trying to calm the nerves that fluttered in her belly. "There is really no polite way of saying what I wish to, so I'm just going to be honest. I'm actually very happy to be stuck here, and even though I know this must shock you, I would like to continue with the party, take part, and enjoy the time that I have left."

Her ladyship's brow rose. "I do not think my house party is the right place for you, my dear. What if it becomes known that you're present? Both of our reputations will be put in jeopardy, yours for innocence lost and mine due to the inability for people to attend incognito." She worked her hands in her lap. "You're unchaperoned and I do not wish to be part of a plot that ends with the ruination of an innocent. I'm ashamed that I even allowed this charade to start in the first place."

"But that is where you're wrong. This is the perfect place for me. If I continue to wear my mask, then no one shall know my identity. And I'm not going to lose my innocence to anyone in attendance, if you're worried about that. There is only one gentleman for me, whom I like more than anyone else. I live in hope you see that his interest will turn toward me too, even though I know I have no chance."

"Is the man in attendance? I really ought to just cosset you away and keep you safe," Lady X said, her gaze weary.

Something in her ladyship's voice gave Lizzie pause and she wondered if the woman already suspected who the gentleman was. Most would after last evening's dinner and the looks Lord Wakely had bestowed on her at times. Glances that were enough to curl her toes in her slippers.

He'd never noticed her in town, or at least she'd never been aware of his notice. "He is in attendance," she said. "The gentleman is a man of the world, has known many lovers, and I have no doubt that if I were not here, he would never look my way. I have nothing other than myself to offer to him, and as it is with most gentlemen of the *ton*, that is never enough. But here, behind a mask, I'm not anyone. It does not matter if I have a fortune or if I don't. It doesn't matter if my family is titled or in trade. The attraction here is based on mutual desire, a connection. I want to experience that and learn all that I can before I have to return to my mother and the life she wants me to lead."

"Hmmm." Lady X tapped her chin. "I will not play coy and deny knowing that you're speaking of Lord Wakely, but it does fill me with some concern. That you like him was obvious last night, and in turn I believe he is quite fond of you too–at least the masked you. But he is a rake, a man who has had many lovers, many who are present at this party. Do you not think it would be best that as soon as I can arrange it, we send you back to the house party you're supposed to be at, and you can start your courtship of his lordship when you return to town? I've never had a guest lose their reputation by being here, and I'm not about to start now. And should Lord Leighton find out you're here he would simply kill me stone dead. I would never recover in society, and neither would you."

"You of all people must understand the restraints that women in our society live by. You would not have started such house parties as these if you did not. Can you not simply for the next few days turn a blind eye? Please, Lady X," Lizzie beseeched.

Her ladyship bit her lip, frowning in thought.

"Do not assume that I misunderstand your concerns, because I don't," Lizzie continued. "I'm simply putting them all aside for a few days. This is my only chance to live a little. Away from everyone. I shall wear my mask and have my maid do me up so I'll never be recognized. I promise you, I shall remain anonymous."

Lady X remained silent, and Lizzie fought not to fidget while she waited for her reply. Would she let her attend the party tonight and the other events like everyone else, or keep her hidden away until she could throw her into the carriage and be rid of her?

"Very well," Lady X sighed. "You may stay, but you're to double your effort in hiding your appearance. An alteration of your voice may be required at times, and whatever you do, do not slip and mention friends or family during conversations." Her ladyship's eyes narrowed on Lizzie. "I am curious to know your age, Miss Doherty. Why is it you're not married yet, my dear?"

"I'm three and twenty." Almost on the shelf by London standards. Not that this was a growing concern for Lizzie; the closer she came to receiving her money the closer she was to escaping her mother, and living a life of her own. She might do as she pleased then, and the *ton* and the men who'd looked the other way when she passed due to her lack of funds could go hang. Lizzie reminded herself that she must thank Hamish again the next time she saw him for saving her from fortune hunters.

"If you stay, do you mean to try your luck with Lord Wakely? I'm not sure your mama has warned you of the risks that you take should you follow your infatuation. No mask will save you from an unwanted pregnancy."

Lady X's words were blunt, and it was a point that Lizzie would have to take into account. If she stayed, and did try her luck with his lordship, she would just have to ensure it stopped at kissing, and maybe a few scandalous caresses. As much as having a child was something she longed for, she did not want one out of wedlock. "I'll not do anything to risk my virtue, in that respect. I know I'm putting my reputation at risk, but it's a risk I'm willing to take."

The thought of having Lord Wakely hold her in his arms, his delectable, sinful lips taking hers, teasing her and leaving her flesh to burn, her blood to pound in her veins, made her stomach clench in delight. "If I was to try and lure Lord Wakely into kissing me, would you know how I could do such a thing? I've never been kissed before, you see."

Lady X let out a sigh, but a small smile lifted her lips. "I can help you, if only to guide you in what you shall wear tonight, how to seduce a man with your eyes and have him eating out of your hand like a little lost, hungry puppy. But anything further than that I'm not willing to do. Are you in agreement?"

Lizzie nodded. "When can we begin?"

Lady X smiled. "We shall begin right away."

FIVE

Later that day Lizzie made her way downstairs. Earlier, her maid had delivered a note from Lady X asking for all the guests to assemble in the parlor. The note stated that the guests had two alternatives for the morning's pleasure, that being billiards or charades. Lizzie had already made up her mind to play billiards as she'd never played charades well in her life.

Before entering the parlor she checked carefully that her mask covered her face and nose and only allowed her lips to be seen. Most guests were already present in the room, and thankfully her step didn't falter the moment she spied Lord Wakely sitting on the arm rest of a settee. A beautiful, dark-haired beauty sat beside him, her body turned toward him in open invitation, but his attention wasn't on the woman, it was on *her*...

A frisson of awareness shot through her as his dark, hooded gaze wandered over her, and she sat in between two gentlemen who were only happy enough to have her join their party of two.

Lady X clapped her hands, gaining everyone's attention.

Today again she wore no mask, and Lizzie had to congratulate Lady Campbell for not following her own rules regarding anonymity. She supposed it wouldn't work for the hostess to be unknown—too much trouble during the events, for starters.

"As you're aware, today's games are billiards and charades. I have taken the trouble of pairing my wonderful guests with partners I think you shall enjoy. As I walk about the room, when I touch you and then the next person, that is your chosen partner."

Lizzie caught Lady X's mischievous gaze and fought not to smile. Would her ladyship partner her with Lord Wakely? After his refusal to kiss her last night she shouldn't want to be around him again, shouldn't want to give him another chance to right his wrong and kiss her.

But it was what she wanted most of all, nincompoop that she was.

The mask ensured her identity remain secret, and the reminder bolstered her confidence. Unless she told him, he would only be guessing if it were her or not. He could not prove it unless he ripped the mask from her face. He wouldn't do such a thing, so she could either run back to her room and hide herself for trying to seduce him last night, or take the few days she had left here and try to have a little fun with him.

The gentleman beside her leaned toward her and whispered his appreciative thoughts regarding her gown. She'd chosen the blood-red silk empire style dress that was extremely low cut across her breasts. The morning gown she'd worn earlier in her room wouldn't do for this house party. Her poor maid had almost had an apoplectic fit when she placed it over her head, but Lizzie adored it.

Yes, the bust was too low. But if she were to play

billiards, and she wanted to seduce a certain viscount who continued to watch her, like the gentleman beside her, the red gown was simply perfect.

Lady X went about the room, touching people on the shoulder. Finally she came before Lizzie, touched her, and then turned and surveyed the room. Lizzie fought back a chuckle as her ladyship strolled before a group of gentleman she hadn't met as yet. The resulting thunderous visage of Lord Wakely's gave her pause.

Did he not appreciate her being partnered with any of them? Did that mean he wished to be partnered with her? Lady X moved on and went toward Lord Wakely. From where Lizzie sat she saw him throw a warning glance at Lady X before she touched his shoulder.

Without moving a muscle, he met her gaze across the room and she shivered at the hunger she read in his eyes. Maybe he wasn't so indifferent after all.

Once everyone was partnered, Lizzie stood and started for the billiards room, not waiting for Lord Wakely. Within a moment he was beside her and placing her arm about his own.

"I gather we're playing billiards then?" he said without looking at her.

"You gathered right. I like the game and play it often, so if we're to play anyone else in our respective games I'm likely to win. How do you play, my lord? Is it adequate?"

"I play adequately at all things," he said, grinning.

She smiled. "Good, because I hate to lose."

The billiards room was as large as a ballroom and sported not one, but three tables. The ten people Lady X had partnered up stood around the centre one, discussing who would play against whom. Lizzie and Lord Wakely joined them and it was soon decided that a couple, who made up one team, would play another couple. Lizzie would go up against the other lady, and Lord Wakely against the other gentleman.

They went to the farthest table from the door and Lord Wakely set about giving them each a cue before placing down the pair of cue balls and one red object ball each. The two men played first and Lizzie sat on a chair with the lady she was to play against. Her female opponent clapped at different times when her partner scored a Hazard or Cannon, but the play was very fierce, both men taking painfully long shots to try to sink a ball or hit each other's. Unfortunately, even though Lord Wakely's effort was admirable, he lost the match.

Lizzie stood, picking up her cue and checking the little piece of leather on the end of her cue was in place to give her enough friction against the ball.

"Better luck next time, my lord," she said, grinning at him. His eyes narrowed and he stayed too close for her comfort, taking hold of her cue and pulling her nearer still.

"Do not crow too soon, my lady, you're yet to prove your worth."

Lizzie clasped her hand about his neck. His eyes widened behind his mask before she whispered against his ear, "I'm worth a lot, my lord. As you will soon find out." Her words were not entirely regarding the game, but herself as well.

She stepped away, checking the placement of the balls and taking stock of her opponent. The poor woman didn't seem to even know how to hit the ball, or hold the cue correctly, and many of her shots didn't go anywhere at all toward her score. Lizzie leaned over the table, took aim, and scored a Canon on her first shot. She looked up and met the gaze of Lord Wakely. He leaned against the wall, arms crossed, but his attention wasn't on the game—it was on her.

Lizzie pushed the distraction that was his lordship from her mind and concentrated. From that point on the contest was really no contest at all. After only minutes, Lizzie sank her opponent's red object ball and finished the game. She clapped, triumphing in her victory. The woman pouted and received a consolation kiss from her gentleman admirer for her effort.

Lizzie placed the cue on the table and went over to join Lord Wakely. She grinned up at him. "Thanks to me, we drew. If you want any tips on playing I'm more than willing to help you."

His lips twitched. "Are you always so amusing?" He led her out of the room and along a large passage that ran along the back of the house. The bank of windows overlooked the rear of the house and the expanse of lawn that surrounded the estate.

"When I want to be, I am. Although my mother thinks to laugh in public is vulgar." A shot of fear went through when she realized that she'd spoken about her family, which she'd promised Lady X she wouldn't do. Her mother was known as one of the worst harridans circulating the *ton*, and mentioning her strict ideals could give her away. If Lord Wakely was even still wondering who she was, of course.

"You're lucky to still have your mother. I lost mine as a young boy. I think I would give anything to hear her chastise me once more." He threw her an amused glance but something in his eyes spoke of pain hidden in their grey depths.

Lizzie didn't know how her ladyship had passed, and she didn't like thinking about Lord Wakely being left motherless as a boy. How sad for him. Her heart gave a little lurch.

"I'm sure your mother would also give anything to be able to do so, my lord. You loved her very much."

He cleared his throat. "I did, but such is life." He seemed to shake himself from the conversation and asked, "Where did you learn to play billiards like that? I think even I could lose to you and I always thought myself adequate enough."

Lizzie preened a little at the compliment. "Father had a table at our home in the country. Whenever my parents left for the Season before I debuted, I would spend the time playing billiards. I used to run competitions with our staff, some of whom are very good players, and I learned that way. It was jolly good fun, and whenever I can sneak out to play when we're home I do so. I usually have to wait for Mama to retire before I can round up the few staff who like to play."

"You play billiards with your servants?" he sputtered, his words laced with shock.

She laughed. "Of course. There isn't much to do in—" She stopped before she gave away where she lived.

He shook his head, chuckling. The sound was deep and sent a frisson of awareness through her. Was he laughing at her second slip of information or at her story itself? That she couldn't answer, and she fought to turn the conversation away from such personal information that could give her away.

She spied a cat asleep in the window and, letting go of Lord Wakely, she went and picked it up, scratching the little animal under its ears before placing a kiss on its head.

"You like cats?" he asked, coming over and giving the animal another scratch.

The black and white moggy purred in Lizzie's arms and

she smiled. "I love cats. When I... that is to say, when I can." She had been about to say 'when I come of age'. Seriously, she needed to remember that she wasn't supposed to advertise who she was. "I'm going to fill my house with them. I simply adore them. What about you?"

He patted the cat's head. "I prefer dogs, but I tolerate cats."

Lizzie placed the cat back down where it had been lying and faced Lord Wakely. The question that had been burning in her mind since last night was too powerful to deny a moment longer. "Why didn't you kiss me last night? And I mean really kiss me, like a man kisses a woman in passion."

HUGO FOUGHT TO FIND A GRAIN OF TRUTH AS TO WHY HE'D DENIED them both what they wanted. The moment he'd seen her enter the parlor this morning, being with her had been all that his mind could conjure. He'd kicked himself for not kissing her, for not giving her what she wanted. He could only blame the last shred of gentlemanly behavior–his friendship with her cousin Lord Leighton–for his actions.

But not anymore. He wouldn't deny either of them what they wanted. In the few moments when he'd thought Lady X would partner her with some other fop, he'd almost had apoplexy before the guests. No one wanted to see a grown man throw a fit over the hostess's choice, but if it meant securing Lizzie as his partner, he was willing to do anything. Even act the fool.

That in itself wasn't normal behavior, not for him, and it was telling indeed.

"I couldn't say as to why I didn't. I wanted to. So much," he said, not able to tell her it was because he knew who she was, and knew her cousin would rip his bollocks from his body should he know he was kissing his relation at a party of ill repute.

But that wasn't the only reason, and this one was the worst of them all. For all of Lizzie Doherty's attributes, she wasn't an heiress and couldn't satisfy the clause in his father's will. Somehow it seemed wrong to kiss her under such circumstances. And even though no one was supposed to know the identity of anyone else at these parties, Hugo would know Lizzie anywhere. Something in the way she trusted him, spoke guardedly with him, told him that perhaps she knew who he was as well.

She leaned back against the wall, reminiscent of his stance as he watched her play billiards. She rocked on her heels, observing him. "Will you kiss me now?"

His body roared with hunger and he closed the space between them without a moment's thought and kissed her. The instant his lips touched hers he moaned. The minute he'd seen her enter Lady X's parlor, he knew they'd end in this position.

Her kiss was untutored, and he clasped her chin, shifting her a little to allow him to deepen the embrace. He nipped her bottom lip and she gasped. It was the perfect opportunity to introduce her to his tongue, which he tentatively touched hers with. In his arms he felt her soften, become pliant. Her hands wrapped about his neck, her body soft and moulded against his.

In this position his desire for her was plainly obvious, but she didn't seem to shy away from it. If anything the minute undulation of her hips told him she was enjoying this as much as he was.

The luncheon gong floated toward them and Lizzie pulled back, her eyes wide with newfound awareness. He grinned. "Did you like my kiss?" he asked, leaning in to bestow another on her before they moved on.

She slowly nodded, her attention snapping to his mouth. What she was thinking was clear to read. It was the same thing he was. How much he'd damn well enjoyed kissing her just then, and not only that, how much he'd enjoyed the morning in her company, playing games and talking about all things, including cats.

He took her hand and pulled her back toward where they came from, heading for the dining room. "Come, we'll sit together for lunch."

CHAPTER
SIX

Lizzie all but floated down the stairs the following day. She'd slept late and broken her fast in her bedroom. The kiss that Lord Wakely had given her had filled her dreams, and today started with the promise of more delicious things to come. Would he kiss her again? She couldn't help but hope he did. At this point in time it was all she wanted in all the world.

The wind howled outside, the storm refusing to dissipate. Lady X had left a note on her breakfast tray that stated the road out of the estate was still flooded, so Lizzie would have to stay another day. It was no hardship, not if it meant that she could continue her seduction of Lord Wakely.

Her stomach fluttered at the thought. If he did suspect who she was, what did that mean for them when they returned to town? Would he wish to see her again, court her perchance?

Lizzie stepped off the stairs and stopped as the man himself strode out of the parlor. He came straight toward her and, taking her hand, towed her in the opposite direction to the room.

"Come, I have a little activity set up for us."

Lizzie fought not to read too much into the fact he held her hand, was seeking her and only her out. They crossed the vestibule and entered a room that would catch the full afternoon sun when it was out. Even with the stormy wet weather outside, the room was still bright, decorated in light pastels and greens.

There were a number of chairs around the room and at each one stood an easel and an array of paints for guests to use.

"I'm going to paint you today," Lord Wakely said, grinning and pulling her toward a chair near the corner of the room which had windows on either side. "Do you paint, my lady?" he asked, helping her to sit and straightening out the folds of her gown to be ready for her impromptu portrait.

"I had lessons as a child, but I was not very good at it. I can sketch better than I paint. Something about mixing the colors just right I could never manage to do well. My paintings all ended up looking abstract and coarse."

"Are you trying to tell me the portrait you'll do of me today will be modern in its appearance?" Lord Wakely sat and positioned his parchment. He gave instructions for how he wanted her to pose and, doing as he asked, she turned her gaze toward the windows and watched the storm bluster outside.

"I am, yes. I'm no Thomas Gainsborough. But I see they have pencils, so I'll forgo the watercolor paint and draw you instead."

He painted her in silence for a time, and for the entire duration Lizzie could feel his gaze, his attention burning against her body like a brand. Every now and then she caught what part of her body he was concentrating on, and her skin heated. "Do you think you've captured the likeness of my breasts well, my lord? You seem quite fixated on that part of my person." She fought not to laugh at his throat clearing. It was very forward of her, but if she was to take this opportunity while she had the guise of anonymity, then she would do all that she could to tease him. Lord Wakely was so very educated in the art of dalliance that it was only during times such as these that she had the slightest chance of matching his skills.

He put the paintbrush down, but she didn't turn to see what he was up to. Her heart thundered in her chest when he stood, tipped her face up toward him, and kissed her. The kiss lingered and without thought she kissed him back. He was impossible to resist, not that she wanted to. She would take all that he could give her while she was under this roof, to a point at least. Her virginity wasn't up for debate.

No sooner had he started their little indiscretion than he sat back down and commenced painting again. Lizzie fought to control her emotions, reminding herself to believe he didn't know who she was and that was why he was interested. The other option—that he did suspect—gave her too much hope, and she wouldn't allow her mind to run away into fantasies of them marrying and having a horde of children together.

"May I ask you a question, my lord?" Lizzie watched an old elm blow in the wind outside and hoped the majestic tree survived this storm.

"Of course." He reached out and adjusted her gown, and she swallowed as his hand lingered upon her leg. "You may ask me anything."

"I'm assuming, by the fact you've not spent any time with anyone else here these past few days, that you're not interested in anyone else. What made you choose me?"

"Then, as I kissed my way down your body, I would hook your legs on my shoulders and kiss you down here," he said, cupping her mons through the gown. Lizzie closed her eyes, biting her lips as he kept his hand there, stroking her.

She moaned, and before she knew it he was kissing her, ravishing her mouth. Her own hand covered his, keeping him touching her, delighting in the feeling his touch brought forth in her.

He broke the kiss, his breathing ragged, his lips red from her kiss. "I would take you with my mouth, lick your sweet flesh until you rocked against my face and found your pleasure."

Lizzie shuddered, her body not her own, but all his. "What kind of pleasure?"

"You'll see..." he said, kissing her again and making her forget who and where she was entirely.

CHAPTER
SEVEN

The following day Hugo lazed in a chair beside the roaring fire in the parlor, his blood as hot as the wood in the grate. Lizzie was literally driving him to distraction. After their interlude in the painting room the day before, where he'd made her climax in his arms, he'd almost ripped both their masks off and stopped all the pretence. But he could not. She was here enjoying a little freedom that was so seldom given to women of her station, and he would not ruin the time she had left by exposing her. He'd wanted for himself one last foray in debauchery, but he'd never imagined those days would be with Lizzie Doherty, a woman who made him laugh and long for so many things he'd not thought to want.

To have a marriage of convenience now didn't hold as much shine as it once did. In fact, it didn't glow at all.

Her laughter carried to him and he looked up, spying the little minx lazing in the window seat with Lord Finley, the man's hands too close to her thigh for his liking. The seductive determination he read in the rogue's eyes was enough to make him seethe, tempted to pummel him to dust.

In the few days they had been stuck at the house party, Lizzie had blossomed into a woman. She should've been gone from these walls the very next day after her arrival, but as luck would have it she was stranded here with them all.

He'd thought she would hide in her room and remain cosseted away like a good girl. Instead she'd thrown herself into the party with a gusto that left him struggling to find his footing. At first, he'd looked at her and had seen a lovely girl, but now...now he saw nothing but woman, a passionate, intelligent woman who made his blood pump fast and hard in his veins. He wanted to be around her, to discuss all manner of things, and he'd not wanted or looked for such things before.

At these parties, the chase, the lure of having someone he'd wanted for weeks, was what had made him attend. He didn't have to worry about courting or conversations, or enjoying himself with anything other than the pleasures of the flesh.

But not anymore. Now he couldn't wait to return to town where he would see Lizzie's face again, this time without a mask.

Hugo sat forward and all but threw his crystal tumbler onto the table before him. He couldn't court her unless he somehow came up with a way to keep his fortune from going back to his uncle. Lizzie's cousin watched over her like a hawk, and if he knew what Hugo had already done with his charge, he'd call him out.

A little voice taunted him that she would never be his, not as poor as she was, and he could thank his father for such a fate. There was little chance he could talk his uncle into allowing him to keep his inheritance, and so because of his need to find a rich wife, something Lizzie was not, he would lose her.

He looked over toward her again and inwardly sighed. He could've looked forward to having her as his wife.

Lady X clapped her hands, gathering everyone's attention. "We're going to play a game. Ladies, I will ask you to leave the room while the men will stay. The gentlemen will spin a top which has an arrow marked on it. Whoever the arrow lands on will bid a woman enter. You will then be required to partake in the most passionate kiss you can create."

Some of the gentlemen laughed, while the ladies giggled and oohed at the game. Hugo met and held Lizzie's across the room, and determination warmed his blood. As everyone went about preparing for the game, he grabbed Lady X's arm. "Can you ensure I'm paired up with the one I want? I'll be most disappointed if she's saddled with any of the other men here present. They should not be honored with her kisses."

Lady X looked at him with amusement. "Oh, and you should? You must take a keen interest, to ask such a thing from me." She let that little statement hang in the air for a moment before she said, "You may ask, my lord, but I do not have to grant your wish. You'll have to wait and see how lady luck plays her hand."

"I'm sure you and lady luck will ensure it's so." He let her go without another word. With Lady X, no one ever really knew if she would help or not should you request assistance. She was an oddity for certain, but hopefully knowing Lizzie was innocent—so much more innocent than anyone else present—she would look out for the young woman. And by God, if he couldn't marry Lizzie, he'd at least taste her sweet lips at any and all opportunities that arose.

Once the room was cleared of ladies, the men sat about a round card table. Lord Benedict, a frequent guest to these types of events, picked up the top and spun it. It landed on Lord Stratford, a man who'd just come into a large fortune and viscountcy. "Seems you're first, lucky sod," Lord Benedict said, smiling and pushing the young buck toward the door.

A lady in a blood-red gown that dripped seduction stood behind the door when Lord Stratford opened it. There was little hesitation between them to touch, and something told Hugo that they'd partnered up already during the house party. They left the room in a flurry of squeals and masculine laughter.

Gentleman after gentleman spun the little top, and lady after lady came in and within only a few moments left with their partner for the night.

When Hugo was the only gentleman left, Lady X gestured toward the door. "You may as well open it yourself, my lord. I'm sure you'll find the woman you're looking for behind the threshold."

Expectation thrummed through him as he strode across the room and wrenched the door open, only to find no one on the other side. Perplexed, he stood there a moment, before laugher sounded behind him.

"It would seem your quarry has escaped."

He sighed. Why had she left? Well, he could probably guess as to why—she had been waiting to be mauled by the opposite sex, without the certainty it would be him doing the mauling, someone she seemed to enjoy kissing. It was only normal that Lizzie would make a hasty exit.

"So it would seem," he said, strolling from the room and

heading toward the back of the house to where the billiards room was located. He would have a hit about for a time, before he retired. He strode past the staircase cupboard, taking no notice of the door being partially opened before a hand reached out and clasped his arm, and tugged him into the small storage room.

Hugo didn't have a chance to react before the softest lips he'd ever felt gently touched his. Desire rocked through him and the breath in his lungs seized. "So, you wished for a kiss after all," he said when she drew away. "I thought when I didn't see you at the door that you'd changed your mind about me."

He felt her smile more than saw it, and, wanting her with a need that left him breathless, he pulled her up hard against his chest. "Can we try that again? Longer this time, perhaps?"

Lizzie ran her fingers up his shoulders and into his hair. "I took a chance and hoped you'd come in this direction. How lucky am I to guess so well?" Her fingers fisted into his locks. "I'm at your leisure, my lord."

No other words were required. Hugo clasped her chin and kissed her, letting her know in no uncertain terms how much he wanted her. She gasped, then her tentative tongue touched his, and he fought for control.

Damn, she was the loveliest woman to have in his arms. She fitted him to perfection, like a pair of perfectly made kid leather gloves. Didn't shy away from his advances and was all too willing participant. His blood pumped loud in his ears and he groaned. How in only a few days had she become his sole purpose? He attended these events to lose himself, to enjoy women who liked games and were free from society's rules while under this roof, but with Lizzie everything was different. His body reacted differently to her touch, her gasps made him yearn to create more. He wanted to please her, make her laugh, and see her bite her bottom lip when he made her embarrassed.

I want her...and not in the biblical way.

"Your kiss is wicked," she gasped, leaning further into his arms, her breasts hard against his chest. Hugo hardened, the delicious ache in his cock fogging his mind. She wanted adventure, not to lose her innocence. He fought his hazy mind to remind himself of the fact.

He clasped her hip and pushed her against the wall. Muffled laughter sounded in the hall outside, footsteps and servants, but none of that mattered. Certainly not at the kind of house party they had found themselves at.

"So is yours. You've placed me under your spell, my lady," he murmured, never having said anything more truthful in his life. Her fluttering hand against his cheek almost undid his resolve to not push her further, demand more of her before they had to part ways, not just here at Lady X's home, but back in London.

"Then do not stop," she said, clasping his lapels and pulling him back to kiss her again.

Lizzie leaned up and kissed Hugo, taking all that he offered her. The hardness that pushed against her belly left her in no doubt that he desired her as much as she desired him. Dizzy with expectation and need, she wrapped herself about him, kissing him with as much force as she could.

Having learned a little during their past encounters, she deepened the embrace, taking a little control back, and his gasp against her lips was payment enough. She longed to hear the sound again. Wanted to be the only woman to ever make him in such a state.

She reached down and clasped his sex, wanting to touch him as intimately as he'd touched her yesterday. The delicious ache between her thighs thrummed and the looks between her cousin and his wife became all too clear.

He hoisted her legs about his waist and pushed them closer than they had ever been before. Still, it was not close enough. She wanted him, all of him, and when he undulated against her sex stars fluttered before her eyes.

Oh yes, this was what she desired. Her heart thumped loud in her ears, and she gasped as he teased them both, giving more pleasure than she'd ever thought possible.

"I wish I knew your name," she gasped, kissing him quickly. "I have an urge to call it out."

He grinned, watching her as he thrust against her sex. "Maybe one day we'll be properly introduced."

Lizzie chuckled. How wicked she was being, and how wonderful it was to be in Lord Wakely's arms while being so. He kissed her again with a fierceness that left her reeling and she clasped his shoulders. The sensations consumed her, and made her wonder how she would ever go on in life without experiencing them again.

And then, like the day before, her body took flight and she shattered in his arms, gasping through his kiss as pleasure rocked from her core to spread to every part of her body.

His breathing ragged, he slowly lowered her to the ground and stepped away. She shivered, already missing his heat.

"May I escort you back to your room, my beautiful lady?"

He took her hand, kissing it quickly before laying it

softly against his arm. Lizzie bit her lip at the sweet gesture. "I...yes. You may."

THE FOLLOWING MORNING LIZZIE WOKE WITH A START WHEN HER maid bustled into the room. "Miss Lizzie, the river will be passable by mid-morning, or so the groundsman has stated, so we must pack up your things and be back at the inn post haste before anyone finds out that you were in attendance here."

Lizzie sat up with a start. Leave? She didn't wish to leave this party, not when she could kiss Hugo in dark, quiet cupboards any time she wished, and not have to be concerned about what anyone saw or thought. Not when for the first time in her life she could freely indulge in passion with a man who was so sensually gifted.

Blast it. But then, if she didn't leave her reputation would be in ruins should anyone find out she was here. And she had been here for a few days now. If Lady X's guests had been stranded due to the river being flooded and the roads being too boggy and wet, it was only rational that others from Lady Remmnick's party would travel to check on her whereabouts. Even now there could be a letter making its way to her mama asking if she arrived safely home after not attending their party. She would have to leave, get back to the inn and pretend that was where she had been all the time.

"Of course," she said, throwing her blankets off and rushing toward her maid, who held an emerald travelling gown. She helped Mary get her dressed as fast as she could, then checked the room once they were packed to ensure she'd not left anything behind. It was an hour of madness.

Putting on her mask, she left her room, then paused outside her door.

The viscount's door remained closed at this early hour. He would probably not wake for some time yet. Disappointment stabbed at her that she'd never see him in such relaxed circumstances again. The past few days at Lady X's home had been scandalous, yes, but awfully fun and carefree. The complete opposite to London at times.

Lizzie pursed her lips, unsure when she'd see Lord Wakely again. Would he wish to seek her out even if their paths did cross, or was their moment of madness these past days simply a little fun for his lordship, and now his dealings with her were done?

That was assuming he'd even recognized her over these past few days. He'd never mentioned her name, but something told her he knew who she was. He was friends with her cousin, so it would certainly explain his instant hovering and keeping his sights on her. Maybe the attraction she thought was between them was simply in her imagination, and Lord Wakely had only sought her out to keep her virtue safe from the other rogues present...but not his, it would seem.

Taking a deep breath, she carried on toward the stairs. In the entrance hall Lady X stood smiling, and Lizzie smiled in return. "Thank you for having me, and I must apologize for leaving with such haste, but, well...I'm sure you understand why."

Lady X walked her outside and toward the carriage. "Of course I understand, dear, and as much as I've enjoyed your company, this is not the place for such a lovely young woman as yourself. But I shall see you in town, where we can converse without those silly masks."

Lizzie clutched her ladyship's hand. "I look forward to

it." She gave the house, where for a time her dream of the Lord Wakely had come true, one last longing glance then stepped up into the carriage. She steeled herself for seeing her mama once again, and the many questions she would face over her whereabouts these past three days.

EIGHT

Upon her return to town, Lizzie found London and all the society balls and parties the same, if not a little tedious and tame after her exposure at Lady X's house party. In the week since she'd arrived back she'd not seen Hugo at all, although the whispers concerning his courting of Miss Fox had doubled and there was talk of an impending announcement of their engagement. Lizzie pushed the disappointing thought aside, not wanting to think about that. The idea of him with another woman, kissing someone else, taking her to his bed, was unbearable to say the least.

Her stomach roiled, and she took a steadying breath to stem the nausea.

"Good morning, dearest. How well you look today," her friend Sally said, sitting down on a chair beside Lizzie's dressing table and pulling off her gloves.

Lizzie frowned. "What are you doing here so early?" She checked the time. "You're not normally up until after luncheon. You must have something extremely important to tell me to be here at this time."

Sally laughed and then dismissed Lizzie's maid. "You'll never guess who rode back into London on his phaeton carriage yesterday afternoon."

Lizzie shook her head, having no clue who Sally could mean, although a little part of her thrilled at the idea it could be Hugo. She'd thought he was back in town already, and giving her a wide berth, but perhaps he wasn't. Just like the rumors surrounding his courtship, perhaps the *ton* was wrong on both counts. Maybe he wasn't after Miss Fox, and perchance he'd been away, and the *ton* was simply making up stories to have something to talk about.

It would certainly not be the first time such a thing had occurred.

"Who?" she asked, checking her hair and finding the design agreeable and thankfully a little flattering. Mary was becoming a very talented lady's maid.

"Lord Wakely. And there is gossip he's ruined a young, innocent miss and will have to marry her."

"What?" Lizzie stood, causing her dressing table chair to fall over backwards. "When did this happen?"

Sally threw her a curious look. "At a county house party, although the details are very sketchy at present, but la. Imagine if it were true? I wonder who the woman in question is."

Lizzie stared in horror at her friend, hating the fact that this ruined woman could possibly be her. She had been so careful returning to the inn, and had been found later that day by Lady Remmnick, who'd been beside herself with worry. But Lizzie had explained that she could not travel to their estate due to the impassable roads, and their own small river that had to be crossed to enter, so she'd simply stayed put at the inn with her maid.

No one other than Lady X knew that she'd been at the

house party. Did others in attendance guess as to her identity? Did Lord Wakely too know who she'd been after all?

Of course, the first day she arrived, having no idea she was at the wrong location, it was possible someone saw her enter the house before she was escorted upstairs to her room where masks awaited her to hide her identity.

Oh dear, this was a disaster! Her mama would kill her and put her into a nunnery should she find out about her little escapade. Any chance of obtaining a suitable, secure husband would also be lost, never mind finding one who would love her. Her chance of marrying with affection would be an unattainable dream due to her own stupidity. She'd be thoroughly ruined!

Lizzie shook the panic that threatened to take hold. Lord Wakely was a rogue, of that she had no doubt. Perhaps after she left he had found someone else to amuse himself with, and this fallen woman, whoever she was, the poor soul, was an innocent. Lizzie rolled her eyes, knowing full well how absurd that sounded. No, the young woman in this latest scandal was her. She was a stupid fool to delude herself otherwise.

"With the dissolute reputation of the viscount, it could be anyone," she said. "He is a rogue after all. Let us not worry any further about it. I'm sure he'll do the right thing and marry the girl and save her reputation, should he have acted so low."

Sally grinned. "Oh, I cannot wait to find out who'll marry such a man. He is awfully handsome and rich, and no doubt would keep any woman happily occupied I would think."

Lizzie started toward the fire, needing its warmth. "Two nights ago at the theater there was talk of his courtship with Miss Fox. The gossip was his uncle in America is set to arrive within the month, no doubt to attend the wedding. I think this new scandalous rumor is a diversion. He's obviously going to marry Miss Fox and add her fortune to his. Maybe they had a tryst and it's becoming public knowledge."

"Maybe you're right. Even so, the next few weeks in town are set to be very interesting," Sally said, her eyes twinkling with mirth.

Lizzie smiled, but pain radiated within her chest. Silly of her, but she'd thought they'd had a connection. His kisses certainly discombobulated her–totally seduced her into the idea of him and her, having a future together. Had she been naive? A silly chit who was imagining more than what was there? Maybe Lord Wakely never knew who she was at all and had simply enjoyed himself with a woman at a party, just as he'd done many times before.

Sally stood and went over to the armoire, flicking through Lizzie's gowns at a rapid pace. "Everyone will be attending the Lefroys' ball this evening, and so too are you. Now," she said, pulling out her favourite gold and silver threaded gown, "this is what you shall wear tonight. The coloring suits your red locks."

"What should it matter what I wear? I have no one to impress." Not anymore at least.

Sally laid the gown on the bed and went in search of gloves. "That has no bearing at all. Everyone who is anyone will be in attendance, no doubt to see Lord Wakely. They'll want to see if his interest in Miss Fox is still founded, or if these new rumors point to another woman entirely."

Lizzie rang the bell for her maid. "Very well, I'll do as you ask, but in all truth, I do not care who his lordship is to be betrothed to. Nor do I wish to see the *ton* take to the

fallen woman, should there even be one, and peck her character apart with their elevated opinions."

"Well," Sally said, picking up her gloves and slipping
them on, "aren't we cutting this morning? Now, make sure
you get some rest today, for tonight shall be a long, exciting
time and I expect you to keep me company until the early
hours of the morning."

Lizzie sighed. "Since you're so keen on my attendance, I
shall meet you at the supper room doors at eight."

"I shall see you then." Lizzie watched Sally turn and
leave just as Mary arrived.

"I'm to attend the Lefroys' ball tonight. Please have a
bath prepared late this afternoon along with a supper tray
brought to my room for an early dinner."

"You do not wish to eat at the ball, Miss Lizzie?"

"I prefer not to eat too much at such outings." And if the
nerves coursing through her stomach already were any
indication, eating at the ball this evening would be nigh on
impossible.

HUGO WATCHED THE ENTRANCE TO THE LEFROYS' BALLROOM LIKE A
man starved of water looked for rain. For the last week
he'd thought of nothing else but Lizzie Doherty and the
time they'd spent together at Lady X's estate. Not to
mention the delectable kisses she'd bestowed. That the
little minx had hightailed it back to London the following
day was not what he'd expected to wake up to find, after a
very restless night thinking of nothing other than her
sweet lips.

He rubbed his jaw, reminding himself it was for the best
that she had left. Their interactions had become more and

more carnal during the days they were together, and a few times he'd had to restrain himself from begging for more.

He'd left for his own estate the same day she departed, determined to move on with his plan of marrying Miss Fox before his uncle could claim his inheritance. Time was running out for him to find a rich wife, and Miss Fox had shown she was open to such an arrangement. Therefore he'd pushed the idea of Lizzie from his mind. They had been at Lady X's house party in disguise, after all, so he could forget the fact he'd known who she was the moment she'd walked into the parlor that day. He'd made no promises, no declarations of undying love.

Whatever love was.

A vision in gold came into view, laughing at something her friend was saying before she curtsied to their hosts and entered the ballroom. His heart did a little tumble in his chest as he took her in, relishing every move, every gesture she made while unaware of his notice.

Taking a sip of brandy, he ignored the tittering about him over his latest scandal. Well, two scandals in fact, but with his reputation, they were nothing new. If the *ton* actually *knew* whom the lady was he was supposed to have ruined, it would be different. How delicious they would find such information. Not that they would care that he hadn't ruined her at all...although he couldn't deny that the thought had crossed his mind numerous times during their few days together.

Never had he felt such acute disappointment as he had the morning he'd woken up and found she'd left the house party. The whole day had turned for the worse from that point on. He'd ordered his manservant to pack his things, and by luncheon he was on the road heading back to his country estate.

He had stayed there for a few days, catching up with his steward and ensuring everything was in order before he headed back to London to see out the end of the Season. Not to mention securing Miss Fox and her thirty thousand pounds before the end of the month.

Now the vixen named Lizzie Doherty glided straight past him without so much as a by-your-leave, and his annoyance doubled.

Not only at her, but himself. He should be glad she wasn't demanding anything of him, allowing him to court Miss Fox and solve all his financial woes. That she did not seek him out left him contemplating the fact that she'd never known the identity of the gentleman who'd kissed her senseless at Lady X's party.

The idea that Lizzie would kiss any man in such a way made his blood run cold. His resolve to remain distant from her, leave her to her own devices, warred with his desire to speak to her again. To be near her and hear her laugh. Her cousin, Lord Leighton, was one of his closest friends, so it wasn't entirely foreign for them to be thrown together at a ball. The *ton* wouldn't read anything more into his being polite to his friend's cousin.

Hugo watched her. She was so very pretty and it was a pleasure to see her once more without a mask. Her laugh caused warmth to course through his blood, and her vibrant eyes simply lit up a room. But she wasn't for him. He needed to marry an heiress with a substantial dowry, and he had to do it soon.

Unfortunately, Lizzie Doherty was a poor relation to Earl Leighton, and because of it, each year she did not find a husband left the possibility of her gaining one decreased. Hugo understood why his father had stipulated such a clause in the will. His father knew of his lifestyle, endless lovers, and spending of funds on the things he valued—horses, gambling, and trips abroad. But now his vices would stop him from pursuing the woman whom he was certain suited him most in this society. Now his own foolhardy past meant Lizzie Doherty was lost to him and he'd have to marry the cold, aloof Miss Fox.

And he *would* marry her, because that was all that was open for him, what he had to do to secure his tenant farmers, his employees across his many estates. Even so, the slow burn that grew as he watched Lizzie wouldn't abate. It hadn't dimmed in the few days since he'd seen her last, and something told him it would not, no matter how much time passed. She'd ignited a fire in his blood that he didn't want to step away from. But how could he have her when taking her as his wife would mean losing everything?

He pushed the problem away to think about another day.

It was a selfish, ruinous, bastard thing to do, but he wanted another taste. He wanted her in his bed, writhing in pleasure. He wanted to kiss every inch of her silky white skin. Suckle her nipples until they coiled into hard little peaks that begged to be licked. Hear her moan his name as she found pleasure on his cock.

He pushed away from the wall and followed her toward the end of the room. She stood with her back to him, gentlemen and women friends surrounding her, and their conversation carried to him as he came closer. Discussions over the latest on-dit.

Him.

He grinned as the conversation halted—all but Lizzie's, that was. Unable to deny himself the feel of her again, he slid his finger along her spine as he came to stand beside her, his own body hiding his inappropriate touch.

"Good evening," he said, catching Lizzie's startled eyes with his own. "You look very beautiful tonight, Miss Doherty." He bowed, clasping her hand and kissing it.

A deep blush bloomed across her cheeks, and he stood back, inwardly laughing that she could kiss him with such passion only a week before, touch and talk to him openly, but feel embarrassment now. That was if she'd even been aware of who he was at the house party.

But something in her manner right now told him she knew he'd been the one with her in the country, and that he knew in return who the vixen was that tortured him with the memory.

Others about them greeted him while some of the ladies present tittered and pulled out their fans, waving them in front of their faces. He turned toward his quarry and gestured to the dance floor. "I believe the next dance is to be a waltz, Miss Doherty. Will you do me the honor?"

She cast a nervous glance at her friend Sally, before nodding, her eyes as wide as saucers. "Thank you, yes."

Hugo led her onto the floor as the previous dance ended. The tremble in her hand gave away her nervousness, and he pulled her closer than he ought. The few days apart had been as long as he'd ever remembered time being. So now, having her in his arms, about to dance a waltz, where they could talk...left him discombobulated to say the least.

Somehow the little wallflower looking up at him with trepidation had captivated his soul.

"Do you like to dance, Miss Doherty?"

She nodded. "I do, yes, when I'm asked." The dance started, and they glided their way about the room. The ball was a crush, but even with the multitude of guests, Hugo didn't miss the curious stares that were being thrown in their direction.

"I do not believe there is a man present who wouldn't wish to dance with you."

She arched one brow, her gaze weary. "You have never asked me before. One might wonder why you would do so now?"

He started and almost lost his footing. She was right too, much to his annoyance. He'd not danced with her before, even though they were often in each other's company. "It's a lapse that I intend to remedy from tonight onward."

"Really," she said, looking over his shoulder. "And why is that?"

He slid his hand a little further down her back, settling it just above her buttocks. He met her gaze, wanting to lose himself in the deep blue depths of her eyes. "Because after what you did with me under the stairs at Lady X's house party, there is little else I think about, other than being with you. Near you. Kissing you until we're unable to stand even that."

Lizzie gasped and stumbled. Hugo hoisted her back into the correct position and continued the waltz. "I see the disguise I was made to wear didn't work with you." She sounded annoyed and he chuckled.

"While I do believe others were unaware of your true self, I was not fooled, no. But then again, I have known you for some time and would recognize your delectable figure anywhere, I should imagine. And your hair, which is a shade not often seen in the *ton*."

"You, sir, are being very forward, and I must admit, rude. You shouldn't speak about me in such a manner."

He scoffed. "Why should I not? What I say is the truth." He pulled her into a tight turn. The memory of having her up hard against the wall, her lithe body full against his, undulating in its own course to gain pleasure, bombarded his mind. He groaned at the thought.

"Are you unwell, my lord?"

"Hugo, please. And no, I'm not unwell, but that does not mean that I'm not in pain." Excruciating pain, and thankfully the waltz still had some music movements to go to save his reputation. The last thing anyone here present needed to see was his engorged cock standing to attention.

"Oh really, and what kind of pain are you in, *Hugo*?" she accentuated his name, mocking it slightly, and the devil sat on his shoulder.

"Do you really wish to know, *Lizzie*?" he asked, accentuating her name in turn. She didn't answer, merely raised her brow.

"Very well, Miss Doherty, I shall tell you. I'm in pain, you see," he whispered, "because from the moment you kissed me, for the handful of days we've been separated, you, my dear, have been the single object of my thoughts. I deliberate on you constantly, longing for a kiss as sweet and thrilling as the last, and I have no shame in admitting that I want you." He leaned closer still to ensure privacy. "I want you in my bed."

He was going to hell for saying such things. Wanting a woman he could not have, not unless she miraculously became an heiress or his uncle refused his mother's money. Neither were a possibility and he shouldn't be here, giving her hope, but he also had to know if what they shared was real, not a figment of his imagination. Was Lizzie Doherty the first woman he actually cared about?

LIZZIE SHUT HER MOUTH WITH A SNAP. HE WANTED HER IN HIS bed! Oh, how scandalous and so very tempting. She grinned up at him, having not thought he'd be so honest with her, but loving the fact that he was. "You wish to ruin me, my lord?"

"Hugo. And yes, thoroughly."

His lordship pulled her into a turn before they headed back down the long ballroom floor. For the last several days, being apart from Hugo had been torturous for her as well. Her body seemed no longer her own, and now in his arms, warmth and throbbing expectation hummed through her blood, and other places as well.

But to walk down this path meant ruination, especially as he'd made no promises to her. Had not offered for her hand in marriage. She would be best to keep him at a distance, see if his desire for her led to more, before allowing anything life altering to happen. Still, that didn't mean she couldn't have a little fun with him in the interim. A stolen kiss here and there never hurt anyone.

"After this dance, *Hugo*, go to the top of the staircase and turn right, then follow the corridor to the very end where you'll come to a room on your left. Enter it and wait for me there."

His eyes widened, and a little triumph blasted through her that she'd been the one to shock him this time.

"And what do you intend to do with me once we're in this room?"

She ran her hand over his shoulder, halting it close to his nape. "Everything. I intend to do everything with you."

As luck would have it, the dance came to an end, and, curtsying while Hugo bowed, Lizzie took her leave of him. She rejoined Sally, who was in a deep discussion about the terrible storm that had come through while she was attending a country house party, the very one that ensured Lizzie had arrived at the wrong location.

"Sally, I have a slight headache and I think I shall return home if you are in agreement. I'll take the carriage and send it back for you for when you're ready."

Sally frowned, taking her hands. "Are you alright, my dear? Do you wish for me to attend you? I do not mind."

Lizzie waved her friend's concerns aside. "No, you stay and enjoy what's left of the ball. It's just a headache, and it will pass. I shall see you tomorrow." She headed toward the entrance hall and had a footman collect her shawl before waiting for the carriage to arrive.

It wasn't long before she was helped up into the equipage and they pulled away from the front of the house and were on their way. What happened next was all a blur, but before the carriage had gained too much speed the door swung wide and Hugo threw himself across the floor before her slippered feet.

"What are you doing?" she gasped, watching as he rolled over, sat up and slammed the carriage door closed. He was rumbled from his little escapade, and when the carriage slowed to stop Lizzie called out to the driver to carry on.

"You're running away from me. Yet again." He looked up at her from the floor, his hair askew along with his cravat, which drooped significantly, leaving his delicious neck visible.

"As much as I enjoyed our time at Lady X's, Lord Wakely, I'm not going to be an easy conquest for you." Despite the fact he was being absolutely adorable by chasing her down, barrelling into the carriage and scaring her half to death. He looked a little shocked by her declaration, and she laughed.

"Where's the fun in an easy conquest? I do not mind chasing you about London if every now and then you throw me a little crumb. Say, a kiss every now and then."

He came and sat beside her, and nerves skittered across her skin. He was so imposing, so worldly, and she was neither. Why on earth he was even in her carriage sitting beside her, she couldn't fathom. The viscount was courting Miss Fox. Cunning and cold was what the *ton* termed the poor woman, even though she was in no way poor. Still, why did he want her?

"Why are you here, Hugo?" she asked, not wanting to be anyone's toy, no matter how well they could distract her with a kiss. She would marry for love and nothing else, and as far as his lordship knew, she was penniless–not something men of their sphere wanted anything to do with. So why did he?

He studied her for a minute, the carriage rocking them gently, the flickering lights of the street lamps illuminating his seriousness every so often. Lizzie didn't say another word, just waited for whatever his answer would be.

"I like you, more than I ever thought I would. Yes, we've known each other in passing due to your cousin, but I've never really seen you before. I feel that in the time we spent together, without society's rules, my eyes were opened and...well, I see you now."

"I will not sleep with you. I will never be another one of your conquests, no matter how much I may have enjoyed our time at Lady X's estate."

He took her hand, pulling her toward him. "When you kissed me, you seemed to have woken me from a dream. An endless cycle of nothings. When I'm near you I feel a sense of calm, but also madness. I knew that if I did not see you again, I would surely become insane."

"You tease, my lord," she said, pulling away. "I do not like games where I'm the playing piece."

"I never tease, no matter what you may think of me or have heard. I always say the absolute truth."

He frowned, and she wondered what he was thinking. If she wasn't a game to him, what was she? Did he even look at her as a prospective bride or was he simply infatuated with her after their weekend at Lady X's house party? Lizzie didn't know the answer to her questions. Was she willing to place herself into a situation where she could be hurt? Not just her heart, but also her reputation. She'd always liked Lord Wakely, and should she allow him to remain close to her, could he possibly fall in love with her and offer marriage?

It was a risk, certainly, but meeting his dark blue-gray gaze, she already knew she would risk everything if it meant she could possibly have this man in her arms as her husband.

"There are rumors about town that you're about to offer marriage to Miss Fox. Is it true?" She had to know, but when he sat back, his attention turning to the streets of London outside the carriage window, a rock of doubt wedged in her stomach.

"Society would have you believe I'm always courting some debutante or matron of the *ton*. But society can go hang, because it's you I want to be close to. Let me, for the remainder of the Season, be with you as much as we can."

Lizzie caught his eyes, willing herself to believe what he said was true, and yet a small part of her wondered at it. Even though she'd seen him at balls and parties with Miss Fox, dancing more than once with her, escorting her to plays and the opera with her parents. Everything pointed to an understanding, and yet, here he was, beseeching her to let him court her.

"I will not deny that I enjoy your company, and you may dance and speak to me at any of the balls or parties that we find ourselves at, but anything more than that, I must decline. If you prove yourself worthy, if what you say is the truth and you're not courting Miss Fox, then by the end of the Season, we'll know."

A muscle worked at his temple and a deafening silence filled the carriage. Had she insulted him? Possibly, but right now she had to think of herself, and the fact that Lord Wakely was a rake could ruin her chances of ever finding a man who'd love her for who she was, not what she had. Not to mention her cousin would not bestow her dowry if she was a fallen woman. Two years and she could live however she liked. Wherever she wanted. To risk her future, whatever direction it moved in, even for a few delightful, very naughty kisses under a staircase was a risk she wasn't willing to take. Not yet at least.

He rapped on the roof and the carriage pulled to the side of the road. "I would never wish to do anything that would cause you harm. In light of what you said, we shall go on as before, friends who socialize. I will not ask any more than that from you even though right now"—he leaned in toward her—"I want more than anything to kiss you."

He was so close that the whisper of his breath flittered across her lips. Without thought Lizzie dampened them and delighted in the fact his attention snapped to her mouth.

"You wish to kiss me?" she said, her words but a whisper, but even Lizzie herself could hear the desire echoing in her voice. Need pulsated between them, invisible and yet linking them like a piece of string. He was so dangerous to her plans. Men like the viscount only had liaisons, married for what they could gain for their pocketbook, not what they could gain for their heart. If she married, and that was a very big if, her marriage would be a love match, and nothing else would sway her. If not, she would die an old, rich spinster who had travelled the world and adopted as many cats as her porter could carry.

"More than anything, but I won't." He sighed, then pushed the door open and stepped from the vehicle. "Are you attending the DeVeres' ball tomorrow evening?"

Lizzie nodded. "I am, yes. Lord and Lady Leighton are chaperoning me. Mama has caught a cold and wishes to remain at our country estate for the time being."

He bowed, shutting the door with a thud. "Well then, I shall see you there. Goodnight."

She called out for the driver to drive on. Oh, what was she going to do with him? However was she supposed to remain chaste, when simply one look from him and she melted like Gunther's Ices on a hot summer's day?

"Goodnight Lord Wakely," she said, laughing when he yelled out on the street "Hugo" before the equipage turned a corner and she lost sight of him.

CHAPTER
NINE

Lizzie stood beside Sally at the DeVeres' ball and watched as Lord Wakely danced a minuet with Miss Fox. What a beautiful woman she was–tall, dark, her skin as flawless as milk. And yet when one came close enough to her, there was no denying that her eyes were as cold as ice.

For a moment she wondered if she'd made the right choice telling his lordship that they could remain friends, but that was all. If he didn't offer for anyone before the end of the Season, then she would know his words were true and maybe they could start anew.

The Marquess of Mongrove bowed before her friend and soon they were off, dancing the minuet as well. Lizzie stood alone for a time before her cousin Lord Leighton joined her, with his wife Katherine by his side.

His lordship offered her a glass of champagne, which she took gratefully. "You look awfully downcast, my dear. Is something the matter?" he asked, frowning a little.

"In all honesty, I am troubled." And if she didn't speak

to someone about it soon she would drive herself insane with her own second guessing.

"What is it, Lizzie?" Kat asked, pulling her toward a small settee that sat along the wall and getting her to sit.

Lizzie took a fortifying sip of her champagne. "I'm sure it has not escaped your notice that no one is courting me. I fear that unless they know of the fortune, my circumstances will not change, and I do not know what else to do. I don't want a fortune hunter, but I also don't want to marry in my dotage." The minuet finished, and Lizzie spied Lord Wakely escorting Miss Fox to her parents, who seemed all too eager to have him with them again.

"As I said six years ago, a man who marries you without a dowry will be marrying you because of how much he loves you, not your pocketbook. Trust that the right man will throw all else aside to have you as his wife. You're worth more than your fortune," Lord Leighton declared, gaining a small smile from his wife.

"I agree," Kat said, taking her hand. "And I must admit that it makes no sense that you've had no callers. Why only last week Lord Lumley enquired about you, and from what I know of that gentleman, he has a fortune of his own."

Lord Leighton stared down at them, a scowl on his face. "Now that you mention it, it is very odd, is it not? Six years since your debut and not one offer. Let me make some enquiries into this and see if I can find out why you're not marriage material."

Lizzie gasped, having not expected her cousin to be so blunt.

"Hamish, that was unkind. Apologize to Lizzie."

His wife's words seemed to pull him from his thoughts and he met her gaze. "Oh, I am sorry, my dear. I didn't mean to make you upset. But women marry men all the time without fortunes, and your family is well connected, so it cannot be that reason. So, there must be something else that's impeding your options."

Lizzie shrugged, then looked up to see Lord Wakely talking to a group of young bucks, one of them Lord Lumley, who her cousin had just mentioned. Hugo met and held her gaze across the ballroom floor, and she shivered. He was so very intense, his eyes all but screamed with heat, and from where she sat even she could feel the warmth.

She tore her gaze from Lord Wakely. "Promise me that if I do not find the right man to be my husband, you'll allow me to do whatever I want with my fortune. After six years gracing Almack's wooden boards, I think it's the least you can promise," Lizzie said, only half joking.

Lord Leighton bowed, grinning. "You may, my dear. I would not deny you your wish."

Lizzie caught sight of Lord Wakely excusing himself from his friends, before he strode purposefully toward them. Butterflies took flight in her stomach and she nodded in welcome. He bowed, taking her hand and kissing it lightly.

"We meet again, Miss Doherty." His lordship shook Lord Leighton's hand and spoke quickly to Katherine.

"Good evening, Lord Wakely. I see you've dragged yourself away from your friends long enough to speak to us. How fortunate we are," Katherine said, grinning up at the gentleman. Lizzie smiled, liking the fact that Kat only spoke the truth, even if it was blunt.

"Ah yes, I have been busy, but I'm here now, and with permission from both you and Lord Leighton I would like to ask Miss Doherty to supper."

Lord Leighton gave his consent and Lizzie stood, seeing no harm in it. They were to be friends after all, she reminded herself. "I would like that, thank you."

Lord Wakely took her arm and they made their way toward where others were going to dine before the other half of the ball commenced. He sat her hand atop his arm and placed his firmly on top, eliminating any chance of escape. Not that she was looking to go anywhere.

Lizzie took in his very fine assortment of clothing that from memory covered a very hard, well-defined body. His black satin knee breeches and white stockings accentuated his legs. His dark blue superfine coat with tails showed off his considerable strong shoulders that could lift her without a moment's hesitation. And had done so beneath Lady X's staircase before he had hauled her up against the wall.

He glanced down at her and held her captive with his eyes, and she fought to remind herself why she'd told him they were to remain friends until his sincerity was proven.

A discreet cough brought Lizzie to a halt, and she dipped into a curtsy when the Duchess of Athelby stood before them, an amused lift to her lips. Sally's mama stood beside her grace, the ladies' inspection of Lord Wakely thorough. Both women were formidable influences within the *ton* and over the past few years Lizzie had come to rely on the duchess's advice whenever she needed a different opinion.

"Your Grace, Mrs. Darwin, you know Lord Wakely. He was just escorting me to supper. Would you care to join us?" she offered, not wanting them to think any more of her being with his lordship than they probably were already. They were friends, and would remain so. The fact that they had shared a passionate kiss meant absolutely nothing.

He bowed, but never ventured to take his hand off hers on his arm. The duchess gave the clasp a marked stare, before raising one perfectly groomed eyebrow.

"Lizzie, I'm so glad to see you tonight. It has been too long. I hope Lord Wakely is being a considerate escort to supper. I would hate to hear otherwise," the duchess said, her words friendly but with a thread of steel lingering within the tone.

Lizzie waved the duchess's concerns away. "Of course he is. We were just talking about how the DeVeres have the best lobster patties available during supper, and how we should rush to ensure we don't miss out."

"I'm sure you have nothing to concern yourselves with. Supper hasn't been announced yet, so you're a little early." The duchess waved a fan idly before her face and Lizzie wished she had one in her keeping, since her cheeks were decidedly warm and getting warmer by the minute.

Mrs. Darwin turned her attention to Lord Wakely, her eyes narrowing in thought. "I heard about town the oddest rumor about you, Lord Wakely. That you're about to be married and that your uncle is already crossing the Atlantic as we speak. Is there something you wish to tell us? We would so love to be the first to know."

Hugo tensed under Lizzie's hold, and not for the first time she wondered herself if he was in fact courting Miss Fox whilst also paying attention to her. But then, they were friends. Perhaps he simply liked her company, since they seemed to get along well enough when together. She had no claim on him, even if she'd dearly love to have one if he were to prove worthy.

"I am not engaged, nor is there any understanding. I'm simply enjoying the Season and looking forward to my uncle's visit. As you know, with my father's death twelve months ago I've had no near family remaining in England."

Lizzie felt a pang of sadness toward his lordship at his reply. She too had lost her father, and even as meddling and annoying as her mother was, at least she still had one parent left. Was Lord Wakely lonely? Was that why he sought the company of parties of Lady X's caliber, where he knew he would have good company both in public and private?

"I'm glad that your uncle is coming," the duchess said sincerely. "We look forward to meeting him when he eventually arrives."

Mrs. Darwin smiled at Lord Wakely before saying, "We missed you at Lady Remmnick's house party, but on our return to London we stopped at a delightful inn and I thought I saw you changing horses. Were you nearby?"

His lordship threw Mrs. Darwin an amused glance and heat rose on Lizzie's cheeks. "I was in attendance at another house party, yes. I hope you found the break from London to your satisfaction?"

The duchess's attention snapped to Lizzie and she raised her chin, not wanting to look as guilty as she felt.

"It was very enjoyable. And your house party, my lord?" the duchess asked, watching them with such inspection that Lizzie couldn't help but feel the duchess knew something was being hidden from her.

"It was most enlightening and pleasurable, your grace." Lord Wakely's clasp on Lizzie's hand tightened, and it shot heat straight to her core. She swallowed, fighting the need to flee, to run away from all these questions.

"Shall we find a table, Miss Doherty?" his lordship asked.

The duchess and Mrs. Darwin moved aside, and they moved on.

"What a stroke of luck that we ended up at the same house party. Did you enjoy the festivities as much as I did? I never asked before." His whispered words tickled the side of her neck, reminding her of his kisses upon the very spot.

"I may have," she answered honestly. In fact, the few times she'd spent in Lord Wakely's arms were something she was never likely to forget. Even now, the pull to be alone with him, kiss him again, touch him and enjoy every nuance that made up who he was, was almost impossible to ignore.

The viscount laughed, covering it with a cough. "*May have?* Are you trying to tell me my seductive wiles are lacking? If so, we can remedy that. You only have to say the word and I'm at your disposal."

Lizzie schooled her features to be less shocked. She bit her lip as the overwhelming feeling she was playing with fire and with a man who was too worldly for her rushed to the forefront of her mind. "Another time perhaps. I see the lobster patties are available tonight. You did mention before that you're desperate to have some again," she said, dissembling.

He pulled her to a stop and caught her gaze. The heat that resonated from his attention made her tremble. What was it about him that brought forth these wonderful but odd emotions to riot inside? His chiseled jaw, perfect olive complexion, and dark hair made him one of the most heart-stopping rogues in the *ton*. And right now his attention was fixed on her. Lizzie swallowed, her gaze sliding to his lips.

"I will hold you to that statement, Miss Doherty."

She nodded, unable to do anything else. How did one

answer such a declaration without giving away just how much she wanted him to hold her to it? And if he did not, she would hold herself to honor what she'd said. For if one thing was certain, she would kiss Lord Wakely again if it were the last thing she did.

CHAPTER TEN

House calls were not something Lord Wakely did. Ever. And yet the following afternoon, Hugo found himself standing before Lord Leighton's townhouse, about to be ushered indoors to partake in an hour of frivolous discussions about nothing of particular interest, other than Miss Doherty, who was of very particular interest to him.

Somehow after their time together in the country she'd awoken a part of him that he'd never thought existed. He was a viscount with a terrible reputation. If he had any desire to hold onto his fortune, he ought to be knocking on Miss Fox's door right at this very moment and courting her. But he could not pull himself away to do so. There was something between him and Lizzie, more than a physical attraction, although that was certainly there as well.

She made him laugh, found situations amusing just like himself. Was happy to have a bit of fun. Her attendance at Lady X's house party was proof of that, but also, the day they'd played billiards, she'd not acted the retiring lady who couldn't possibly play a game generally only men would partake in. Not only had she stepped up to the competition, but she'd been an exceptional player and had looked delightful bending over the table.

Lizzie had a direction for her future. Whether that included a husband would be anyone's guess, but something told him she would be perfectly capable of living the spinster life and becoming quite fond of it. Miss Fox had never been very particular toward him—she showed as much interest in him as he did in her, and it gave him pause. Lizzie had showed him there could be so much more between a husband and wife, which drove home just how much he'd want his marriage to resemble that of his friends' love matches.

He needed to kiss her again, if only once, to know if his desire for her was simply a one-off emotion or if each time they kissed he'd want nothing more than to do it again.

If what he suspected was true, and Lizzie would suit his character much better than Miss Fox, he would petition his uncle to forgo the inheritance that was set to revert to him at the end of July. Surely the love his uncle had for his sister, and for her child, would outweigh his need of money.

Hugo rapped the knocker on the front door and it opened without delay. He strode into the entrance hall, handing the footman his coat and gloves. An elderly butler stepped forward and bowed.

"Lord Wakely, if you would be so kind as to follow me, the at home is being held in the front sitting room today."

Hugo followed the old retainer, bracing himself for a flurry of gasps and gossip when he entered the room. The butler announced him, and Hugo halted just beyond the threshold as an army of startled female eyes, gaping mouths, and amused expressions met his appearance. He took in the room, seeking out Miss Doherty, and inwardly cringed at seeing her mother seated beside her. When had she returned to town?

Hugo steeled his resolve. He'd faced worse challenges in his life—a room full of women and a bedevilling mother was nothing to be terrified of.

Mrs. Doherty stood and curtsied. "Lord Wakely, welcome. Please, come be seated by us," she said, gesturing to a vacant chair before them.

Hugo did as she bade, welcoming a cup of tea that Miss Doherty handed him, her small smile of welcome warming his blood.

"We're very happy you decided to join us this afternoon, are we not, Lizzie?" Mrs. Doherty said, sitting back down and smiling between them both.

Lizzie took a sip of her tea. "You are most welcome, Lord Wakely." Her welcome was benign enough, but Hugo could hear that she actually meant her words and was pleased to see him. A little warning bell went off in his mind that he was toying with her, giving her false hopes where there might be none, and yet he couldn't stay away from her. He'd never reacted to anyone in the way that he reacted to Miss Doherty. No matter the consequences, he had to see if their chemistry was a figment of his imagination or something he could discuss with his uncle, beseech him to leave Hugo with the funds that should rightfully be his in any case. If his uncle would allow him to choose a wife he felt some affection towards, not one who had a fortune and would marry him before the month was out.

"Did you enjoy the ball last evening, Miss Doherty? I heard this morning that it ended after dawn."

Lizzie laughed, and her eyes brightened with amusement. "I did, my lord, and I can assure you, as I was one of the last to leave the entertainment, that it did indeed end as the sun kissed the morning sky."

"You did not stay, Lord Wakely?" Mrs. Doherty asked.

Hugo shook his head. "Alas no, I had another engagement to attend." And not one that he wished to elaborate on here and now, or ever, if he were honest.

Lady Leighton came over and stood behind Lizzie's chair, joining their conversation. "You attended Miss Fox's soiree, I understand," she said, her words tinged with an edge of reproach.

Hugo smiled, taking a sip of his tea. "That's right, and the event was overcrowded. I did not stay long." Only long enough to dance with Miss Fox and then depart. Lady Leighton watched him, and he fought to remember if she had been in attendance. Did she know he had danced with Miss Fox? He was a cad, keeping his options open in such a way. Panic tore through him that what he was doing was wrong. Not just to Lizzie, but to Miss Fox also, and he couldn't continue down this line of untruths.

If he told Lizzie his predicament, would she understand? If only he could get her away from here, talk to her privately.

"If you would excuse me. My friend Sally has just arrived, and I need to speak with her."

Hugo stood when Lizzie did and, bowing, watched her leave him with her mother and cousin by marriage. He placed down his cup of tea, not wishing to stay with Lizzie occupied elsewhere. "It is time I left as well. Thank you for the tea, Mrs. Doherty, Lady Leighton. I shall see myself out."

"Good afternoon, Lord Wakely," her ladyship said, her tone no better than before.

Hugo left, and while making his way to the entrance

hall found Lord Leighton hanging about the staircase. "Hugo," he said, coming over and shaking his hand. "It's good to see you. Come, I need to speak to you. We can talk in my library."

"Of course." Hugo followed, wondering if Hamish's wife's cold manner toward him was the reason for this sudden tête-à-tête. Hamish gestured for him to sit and Hugo made himself comfortable. Thankfully, instead of tea, Hamish handed him a glass of brandy before seating himself behind his desk.

"I won't mince my words, as I'm sure you're aware of why I asked to talk to you privately today."

Hugo took a sip, not willing to give way that easily, although Hamish was one of his oldest friends, so he wouldn't dissemble for long. He wouldn't lose his friendship over the predicament that his father had placed him in.

"You've been seen a couple of times around Lizzie, and your appearance here today makes me wonder what your sudden interest is about. Are you courting her?"

Hugo ran a hand through his hair, searching for how best to explain himself. "In all honesty, I'm not sure why I'm here at all. And I'm sorry if that offends you, I mean no disrespect, but when it comes to Miss Doherty I can't seem to keep away. Even though a marriage between us may be impossible."

The earl leaned back in his chair, his stoic visage giving away little other than annoyance. "You can never marry her why?"

Hugo sighed, hating his father more than he ever had before in his life, and there were plenty of times he'd hated the man dreadfully. His father had never taken to him as a child. Hard and painfully correct in all things, he'd pushed

Hugo to do as he did. Of course, Hugo had never taken after his father, had been a free spirit like his dearly departed mama, and had rebelled. So much so that his father had won the final battle and ripped his inheritance away from him in his final blow from the grave.

"You know my uncle is on his way to London. Well, everyone in London believes it's so he may attend my wedding to Miss Fox, who I'll apparently offer to very soon. That is not the case. He's arriving to take control of the money my mother brought to her marriage to my father. My sire has felled his final blow against me from six feet under and stipulated in his will that I'm to marry within twelve months, and to an heiress of no less than thirty thousand pounds. If I do not, the money goes back to my mother's family. I only have a few weeks before the deadline, and because I've not married as yet, my uncle now assumes that I will not—hence his arrival."

Lord Leighton let out a whistle, his eyes wide in shock. Hugo nodded. "So, you see, I shouldn't be here and yet I also cannot stay away."

"Lizzie is my cousin, and under my charge whenever her mother leaves town. Katherine and I care for her deeply, look out for her just as if she was one of our own children. You know she has no dowry and therefore cannot meet the stipulation in your father's will." Lord Leighton stood, coming around the desk and taking his glass. He refilled them both before handing his back to him. "As much as I sympathize with your predicament, I cannot allow you to continue to court Lizzie, or give her any hope. She deserves a marriage of love and I'll not have her marry anyone, not even you, my friend, if there is no affection. You may be as you've always been—distant friends, people who move within the same set—but do not venture any further from those rules. I would be most displeased if you did."

The thread of steel in his friend's voice brooked no argument. Hugo could understand. Hell, should he be in Hamish's situation right now, he would say the exact same thing. But the thought of removing himself from Lizzie's sphere, courting Miss Fox, and entering a marriage of convenience wasn't what he wanted. Not anymore. "Of course, I shall do as you bid. Allow me some grace in pulling away from Miss Doherty. She's innocent in all of this, and if I can I will try to limit the hurt I may cause by ceasing my interest." The thought of not being near her left a hollow void in his gut.

"Of course. I wouldn't expect anything less. Now," the earl said, downing his drink. "I had better make an appearance at my wife's at home or I shall be in the doghouse."

Hugo stood, placing his crystal glass on the desk. "I'll see myself out."

He left, climbing up into his carriage that stood waiting at the front of the townhouse. This was for the best. Lord Leighton was right, and he'd been wrong in his dealings with Lizzie Doherty. It was a cold comfort knowing he would never hold her in his arms ever again.

A week later, Lizzie hadn't seen or spoken to Lord Wakely. Not since she saw him leave her cousin's townhouse looking like the sky had fallen and he was trapped beneath it. Katherine had let it slip that the viscount had spoken to Hamish prior to leaving, and not for the first time she wondered what that conversation was about.

They were friends of course, so it could've been about

anything, but something told her it had involved her. And whatever her cousin said had made Lord Wakely leave in much lower spirits than when he'd arrived.

Tonight she was attending the Duncannons' annual ball. Across the room she spied her friend Sally, who waved and started toward her, weaving through those who stood between them.

"Lizzie, how lovely to see you again. I had hoped you would attend tonight. The gossip throughout London is all about Lord Wakely and his sudden arrival at Lady Leighton's at home last week. He left just as I arrived. How long did he stay for?"

"I have heard I'm the latest on-dit, and truly, he didn't stay long enough to cause all this drama. And since his departure, we've not seen him again," Lizzie said, hoping to put to rest any gossip, although by the curious looks she was gaining from those in attendance tonight, her wish didn't look to be coming to fruition.

"Come and sit, it'll be more comfortable a little away from this terrible crush." Sally pulled her toward a couple of vacant chairs and sat, tapping the chair for Lizzie to do so also.

"I heard that the viscount came and spoke to you and no one else, and that after he left he was seen entering Lord Leighton's library. Do you think he's going to offer for you?" Sally clasped her hand, her excitement over the prospect of Lord Wakely asking for Lizzie to marry him too much to stifle.

"Sally, I need to tell you something, but you must promise not to tell another living soul. Ever. If you speak a word of what I'm about to tell you I will be ruined in society forever."

Sally's eyes widened and for a moment she didn't say a

word, before she crossed her fingers. "I will never tell anyone. Not that I need to promise such a thing, as I would never break my trust with you, but you may be assured I promise never to tell another living soul."

Satisfied, Lizzie ensured they were alone before she told her friend all of what had happened at Lady X's estate–how she came to be there and what happened over the ensuing days. Never had she seen her friend without words, but it would seem that after hearing every little detail Sally Darwin was totally mute.

"Say something, please, anything. Your silence concerns me."

Sally let out a sigh before she said, "And now that you're back in London, what is it exactly that's between you? He's most definitely seeking you out, but you do know that he's still being seen in the presence of Miss Fox? I don't have to tell you that Lord Wakely is known within the *ton* as a bit of a rake, easily led and not the most trustworthy when it comes to the female sex."

"Lord Wakely and I have decided to remain friends and that is all. I'm mindful of him, do not despair, I'm not blind. Especially with his courting of Miss Fox, which was quite ardent prior to what happened in the country between us. It leaves me wondering if he's in need of funds."

"He's wealthy though, my dear, so that cannot be the reason. He either wishes for more coin to add to his coffers or perhaps he holds some affection for her." Sally frowned toward the dancers and guests milling about them. "Or there is something we do not know and that he isn't telling anyone. I did hear that his uncle is coming over from New York. Maybe something is afoot in his family."

Lizzie couldn't help but chuckle at Sally and her wayward thoughts. She had always had a great imagination and saw possibilities of things where Lizzie could see none.

"Whatever it is, I have no dowry, and although my cousin is titled, my own family line is not. Unless someone falls in love with me, I will not marry." And when that special someone did fall in love with her, then and only then would they find out just how wealthy she was. Otherwise she would gleefully buy her own townhouse, take in any stray cats that needed a home, and be quite content with the situation.

"Whatever has happened between you, either in the country or now back in town, the one question you should be asking yourself is if you like him enough to try and help him on. Turn his attention to you fully, so that he'll forget Miss Fox and her fortune and want you instead. It's happened before—it can happen again."

Lizzie doubted it would happen to her, but the thought had crossed her mind. How she would love to have Lord Wakely to wake up beside every morning, be the whole center of his affections. She sighed. "And if I throw myself at him and he still marries Miss Fox? What then?" Well, then she'd be unmarriable. Was the risk of being in Lord Wakely's arms again worth it?

Sally clasped her hand, gaining her attention. "No one need ever know you set out on this course. Not if you're careful. Lord Wakely could be the other half to your soul. Don't you think seeing if that is true is worth the risk?"

Lizzie didn't know what to do. It was such a gamble. Could she encourage his lordship into kissing her again, being more than friends as they had agreed? Remembering their time at Lady X's, and then again when he was in the carriage with her in town, something told her it wouldn't be that hard at all.

"He is rumored to be arriving tonight. A perfect opportunity to put your plan into action."

"Your plan," Lizzie said, smiling. Hope blossomed within her and excitement thrummed in her veins at the thought of seeing him again. "Do you know what, Sally? I think I shall throw caution aside and see what will happen. I'm sick of sitting about, waiting for my true love to find me. Maybe he needs a little help. A little push."

Sally nodded. "I agree. And if I'm not mistaken, your quarry has just entered."

Lizzie bit her lip, looking toward the ballroom doors. Lord Wakely stood on the threshold, bowing to their hosts, and all she could do was take in his glorious beauty. His dark, wicked looks, his striking height and immaculate evening dress. Nerves pooled in her stomach. It was one thing to kiss a man with a mask on, thinking no one would know who you were, but it was another thing entirely to kiss him without any pretence. But if it meant that she would kiss Lord Wakely and possibly find he was the man for her, she would. It was a pleasurable sacrifice she was willing to commit, and maybe even commit tonight.

HUGO SURVEYED THE DUNCANNONS' BALLROOM FLOOR AND spotted the very bane and sole center of his attention sitting next to her closest friend. Both women seemed to be enjoying the ball, but their conversation appeared to be keeping them separate from everyone else and, if anything, appeared a little secretive.

Hugo found himself grinning and making his way into the room. He started in Lizzie's direction, wanting to see her again no matter that only a few days ago he'd promised

Hamish he'd stay away. But tonight Lord Leighton was attending another ball, and therefore wouldn't know Hugo was about to ask his cousin to dance.

He bowed before Lizzie and Miss Darwin, who stood and curtsied. "Good evening, Miss Doherty, Miss Darwin. I thought I might ask Miss Doherty to dance. The waltz is up next." Hugo held out his hand, waiting for Lizzie to take it.

She looked at it for a time, her eyes wide, before placing her hand in his, allowing him to escort her out onto the ballroom floor. The room was a crush, and instead of going out to dance, he led Lizzie toward the terrace doors. With so many in attendance, very few paid them any attention of the direction they were heading. Before anyone could take note he whisked Miss Doherty outside, to stroll along the flagstone courtyard.

The night air was warm and in the distance the sounds of London and its life echoed through the night. Other couples strolled as well, and Hugo led Lizzie away from them to ensure privacy.

"I have not seen you for some days and I apologize for that. My time has not been my own with my uncle's expected arrival some time in the next few days. There are other things that have taken up my time, but I had to see you again." How he wished he could tell her why he should not be before her, wanting her as much as he did. He fought not to lift his hand and place a little strand of her hair off her cheek. He wanted to touch her, kiss her, make her his.

"The Season is busy, you don't need to explain anything to me." She took a couple of steps away and studied the shadowed garden before them. A bird cooed in the dark and a small smile lifted her lips. How beautiful she was. How had he never seen it before? If only he'd not been so involved satisfying his own pleasures, he might have made

Lizzie his wife years ago and his father would never have done what he did.

"I want to kiss you," he blurted out, unable to take his words back. Nor did he want to. They were the truth. He wanted her, and upon his uncle's arrival he would beseech him to ignore his father's will, allow Hugo to keep his inheritance and marry Miss Doherty who had not a penny to her name.

She didn't turn to look at him and her strong resolve made him adore her even more.

"I want to kiss you too. In fact, I've thought of little else since I left the house party."

Her words were a blow to his gut and he moved closer, sliding his hand along the balustrade to the point where they just touched. The moment his finger touched hers it shot a bolt of longing so strong and fierce it threatened to knock him off his feet.

Hugo looked behind him and noted there were fewer couples than before, but the terrace doors remained open and hundreds of people were only a few feet from where they stood. Anyone could walk out at any time, and yet, he had to taste her. His body was blocking a lot of the guests from seeing Lizzie. Maybe a chaste kiss would be possible, if they both desired it.

"Kiss me," he said, laying his hand atop hers, linking their fingers. "No one will see."

Lizzie glanced behind him and then, when he thought she'd thought better of his idea, she leaned up and quickly but quietly kissed him. The chaste touching of their lips wasn't enough, and even though he tried to deepen the embrace, she pulled away, again checking to see if anyone saw.

That there were no cries of scandal told Hugo no one had witnessed them.

"Tell me something, anything, to stop me from ruining us both and taking you in my arms in front of all the *ton*." Hugo straightened, holding his arms behind his back.

"What would you like to know?" she asked, tilting her head to one side.

"Everything I do not know already."

She turned and leaned against the balustrade, watching him. "Well, I'm on the shelf, but you already know that. I'm three and twenty and have very little to recommend but myself. I enjoy horse riding and travel, and I volunteer at the London Relief Society for the Duchess of Athelby and their set. I have no siblings and my mother is controlling and pushy. Not that I should speak about my parent in such a way, but yet it is true. I love cats and will tolerate dogs."

Hugo barked out a laugh. "How can you only tolerate dogs? They are the best of company. They never judge, and will give unconditional love."

"Hmm." She shrugged. "But they're awfully pouty, I find. Always wanting affection and reaffirmation about what a good boy or girl they are. Whereas cats, well, they're independent, strong, wilful, and do not care what anyone thinks. I suppose I strive to be very similar to the species. I no longer wish to care what anyone thinks of me."

"Really?" Hugo wagged his brows. "Is that true? For some, should they know we're outside having an indiscreet tête-à-tête, would have a lot to say about you. In fact, you'd probably end up in one of the gossip rags that will come out next week."

"I'm willing to risk all if it means that I get what I want." She met his gaze and the dark determination in her blue orbs fired his blood. Did she mean him? Did she wish to fight for him?

Her words strengthened his resolve to beseech his uncle to leave his mother's money well alone so he could marry her. The idea of starting a life with a woman who not only stimulated his mind but his body calmed his soul.

"My horses are in need of a good run. I'm taking the gig out tomorrow, a couple of hours in the country to see how they perform. Would you be willing to accompany me?"

"Alone?" she asked.

He nodded. "If your mama will allow."

"There is no impediment if you have a driver and groom with you to act as chaperones. Mama will approve such an outing."

"Eleven then," he said, watching as she pushed away from the balustrade and headed back into the ballroom. He followed her progress, enjoying what he saw. Tomorrow he would have her to himself for a couple of hours, where they could talk freely and maybe continue the delightful kissing that had brought them together to begin with.

CHAPTER
ELEVEN

L izzie woke with a start, and sitting up, she jumped out of bed. The day trip into the country with Lord Wakely beckoned and she couldn't wait to see him again.

Last night, after she'd kissed him, chaste as it was, she was left longing for more, and with the realization that she wasn't willing to allow his lordship to marry anyone else but her. The uncontrollable feeling of floating whenever she was about him, the desire to see his eyes darken in hunger, was something she wasn't willing to lose. Not to a Miss Fox and her thousands of pounds in any case. That woman could marry whomever she pleased, and it did not please Lizzie for her to marry Lord Wakely.

At the allocated hour she paced the hall of Lord Leighton's home, watching the traffic for his lordship's gig. Right on time, his driver accompanied by a groom pulled up before the steps with four matched horses. The gig was not any run-of-the-mill vehicle, but a barouche box.

After helping her climb up, he gave her a small blanket to place over her legs, and they were soon heading out of

London on the great north road. If only they continued on the road, they could travel all the way to Gretna Green.

What a delightful adventure that would be.

"Are you well, Lizzie?" he asked, throwing her a small smile.

She reached up to hold onto her bonnet. "I am. Very well, thank you. I'm also very excited about our outing today. Thank you for inviting me."

"My pleasure," he stated, meeting her eyes.

"So, where are we going today? Is there a plan?" On the seat opposite them sat a basket, and she hoped that it held a picnic. How wonderful if he'd thought to do such a thing. She'd never had a picnic before with a gentleman.

"We will drive a little ways, to let me see how my matching pair go under the guidance of another, and if we find a nice place to stop, we'll have a picnic. I hope you're not averse to eating outdoors."

Lizzie shook her head. "On the contrary, I love doing things like this." She looked about for a time, before saying, "Are you looking forward to your uncle arriving? You said he was due any day."

He didn't reply at first, but kept his attention on the scenery. Then he said, "In all truth, my uncle's arrival isn't a happy prospect. He's here to ruin me, if I'm to be honest with you."

Lizzie gasped, having not expected that answer. Did he really mean what he said? His uncle was coming to ruin him? What did that even mean? "I don't understand, my lord. Why would he wish to do that? Wasn't he your mother's only brother?"

Lord Wakely sighed, rubbing his jaw, which Lizzie noticed had the slightest shadow of stubble. Her hand itched to feel it, to see if it would prickle against her palm, but she did not. First she wanted to know what was going on.

"He is all that I have left of family, but it's not his fault he wishes to ruin me." His lordship paused for a moment, the line between his brow deep and furrowed. "My father, as you would remember, passed away just under twelve months ago. When alive, it was no secret within the *ton* that we disagreed on many things, one of which was my lifestyle. I wasn't the best-behaved gentleman running around London."

He threw her a bemused glance, and Lizzie chuckled, having seen that herself. She'd also pined over Lord Wakely while he'd enjoyed his life to the fullest, often dreaming she was his quarry, to be flirted with and seduced. "I have heard of your antics."

He turned and grinned at her before looking back to the driver as the man maneuvered the carriage to the side of the road to allow a mail carriage to pass in the opposite direction. Their driver yelled out a salutation to the other driver and then pulled back into the centre of the road.

"What I didn't know was that my father would strike at me one final time, from the grave. He stipulated in his will that I am to marry within twelve months of his death, to an heiress who comes with a minimum of thirty thousand pounds. If I do not, the money my mother brought to the family upon her marriage will revert to her brother living in New York. And, as you can see," his lordship said, gesturing to himself, "I have not married, and my time is almost up, hence my uncle's imminent arrival."

Of all the stories that Lizzie had heard, she'd not expected this one. Lord Wakely would not be penniless unless he married an heiress, however he would find it hard to keep up his present lifestyle without selling off some of his property. Well, at least it explained why he'd been courting Miss Fox these past months, even if sporadically. And why he was reluctant with her, only too willing to remain her friend and nothing else. There would be many reliant on Lord Wakely for a living, not just the servants who worked in his homes, but also those who worked his lands. The loss of his mother's money would be devastating for so many. Even so, Lizzie was an heiress, not a penniless miss. But Lord Wakely did not know her secret, so should he choose her in light of his current situation, it could only mean one thing. He cared for her. A great deal.

"Why are we out driving together then, Lord Wakely? Shouldn't you be with Miss Fox instead? She after all meets your father's last wish." Lizzie kept her eyes on the road, wondering what he'd say to her statement.

"I ought to be, yes, but I'm not, and there's one simple reason why that is so."

At that she couldn't continue looking away. Gazing up, she met his gray orbs and lost herself in their depths. "And that is?"

"I don't want Miss Fox."

His words rocked through her and she clasped the seat to steady herself just as a large drop of rain fell and splashed on her cheek. The single drop was soon followed by a deluge. "Oh my God, Lord Wakely, it's pouring." Lizzie laughed as they were soon drenched, her perfectly coiffured hair now limp about her shoulders, her day gown of light blue muslin soaked and clinging to her like a second skin. The driver pulled up under some trees and Lord Wakely asked his groom to help him with the barouche's collapsible hood. He cursed when the blasted thing wouldn't budge.

"It's stuck," he said, looking about for other shelter.

Lizzie held her shawl over her head, but it too was soon soaked and of no use.

"Over there," he yelled through the rain. "I see a barn." Lord Wakely turned to the driver and groom while opening the carriage door. "I'll take Miss Doherty over to the barn to shelter from the storm."

"Right ye are, my lord," the driver said, nodding slightly.

The barn was a large wooden building with two double sliding doors at its front. Inside, stacks of hay lay about from last year's crop. A few pigeons flew about as she entered, otherwise the space was free of animals.

Lord Wakely joined her, taking off his coat and hanging it from a nail he found on the wall. "We'll stay here until the rain has passed and then I'll return you to town. Your mother will not be pleased you're returning damp." He slid the doors shut, cocooning them in the dry space.

Lizzie laughed. "Damp? I'm drenched through." She went up to where the hay was stacked and sat, pulling off her half boots and stockings to dry. "The storm must have been behind us. I never saw it coming."

"No," he said, coming to sit beside her, taking the opportunity to pull his boots and stockings off as well. "Will you call me Hugo like you did before, when we're in private? I'd much prefer it to my lord or Lord Wakely."

Chilled as she was, warmth ran across her skin at his request. "I would like that. You may call me Lizzie in return."

He reached up and pulled a piece of hay from her hair, throwing it away. Their gazes locked, and no matter how much she tried Lizzie couldn't look away. Unlike the first time they kissed, the lead up to this one seemed like an excruciatingly slow dance.

Hugo leaned down and, clasping her jaw, kissed her. His lips were soft, and although they were cold from the rain outside, with one touch any trace of chill fled. Lizzie kneeled, running her hands over his shoulders to clasp about his back. She kissed him back with all that she was, showing him with her touch that she was his match in every way.

His kiss deepened, and Lizzie matched his desire. How she'd wanted to be with him like this again, how for night after night she'd lain awake with images of being in his arms, having his mouth hot and passionate against hers.

Her skin heated, her cold damp clothes forgotten as his hands skimmed down her back. "Touch me," she gasped through the kiss.

He pulled her hard against him, and, still kissing, they flopped onto the hay. Hugo lay beside her, his hand running over her waist and down over her hip, sliding around to clasp her bottom.

Lizzie gasped as he lifted her leg and laid it over his, placing him so very close to her aching core. Wanting to feel him, all of him, she shuffled closer and the hard line of his desire pressed against her abdomen, so solid and big that she couldn't help but wonder how it all worked. Wanted to know with a desperation that matched her desire.

He clasped her hand and took it down between them to lay it on himself, his dark hooded eyes watching her. The need coursing through her was addictive, and at that very moment Lizzie understood that Lord Wakely was for her. Only with him did she trust enough for such kisses, such touches. Never before had she reacted to any gentleman the way she reacted to him.

"Touch me as well," he begged, his voice hoarse with need.

She did as he asked, taking his hard member into her hand through the fabric of his breeches and feeling its length. He pushed it against her hand, moaning against her lips as he kissed her with a ferocity that left her breathless. "Do you like that, my lord?"

He growled, nipping her lip. "You can see that I do."

Heat pooled between her legs and following his lead she clasped his arm that gripped her leg and put it against her most private of places. A place that no one but him could touch. She ached with the need of him, to stroke and slide his hand, give her pleasure just as he had at Lady X's house party.

He gathered up her gown, pooling it against her stomach, and then without hesitation, without caution, laid his hand against her mons. Lizzie shut her eyes as unbearable pleasure ran through her. He stroked her flesh, teasing her with a tentative touch that wasn't enough. She needed more, beyond anything she could ever understand.

"Touch me like you did at the house party, Hugo." She wrapped her hand about his member, squeezing it a little, and he gasped. "Make me feel what you did before."

"I want you. I want you so much," he said, sliding his hand between her wet folds, circulating his thumb on a spot that made her blood turn to molten lava. She moaned, kissing him, increasing her own touch. She broke away to look down at his breeches, then, ripping at the buttons on his front falls, reached in and touched his flesh.

His skin was so soft, like velvet, and he was hers. All hers. The smallest amount of liquid pooled at the tip of his phallus and she wiped it off with her thumb. His fingers undulated against her core and she moaned, wanting more. Her skin burned beneath her wet gown. Her breasts ached, her breathing shallow as he continued to tease her.

"This isn't enough," he gasped, pushing her onto her back and coming to kneel between her legs. Lizzie licked her lips, wanting him with a need that frightened her. She didn't want to think about the fact that she could lose him if he decided that money was more important than his feelings, and yet she could not push him away.

"I'll not ruin you. I promise. Just trust me."

Lizzie watched as he pushed his breeches down. His manhood jutted out, long and thick, and she swallowed. A part of her wanted to run, get away from such a sight, and yet another part of her wanted nothing more than to see what he would do with it.

He came down over her, placing himself against her flesh, and then he slid, sending stars to form before her eyes. The little bead of moisture she'd felt before mixed with her own desire, teasing them both toward a climax she longed to feel again.

How was such a thing so enjoyable? She spread her legs wide and, wrapping her arms about his shoulders, kissed him deeply. He moaned, and wanting more she pushed against him, undulating and seeking her gratification.

"Oh yes, Hugo," she gasped as spasms of pleasure thrummed through her core and throughout her body. With every push against her flesh another bout of fulfilment went through her and she moaned.

His kiss turned scalding and Lizzie didn't shy away from his frenzied state. She wanted him to be crazy for her, to want her as much as she'd always wanted him. He gasped, calling out her name as heat speared across her belly.

They lay spent in the hay together for some time, their breathing laboured as they tried to regain their equilibrium. Hugo slumped beside her, and after a little time pulled out his handkerchief, wiping away his seed. He gathered her dress and settled it back over her legs.

"It's official, I now am a rake of the worst kind."

His voice held no amusement. Lizzie turned toward him, taking in his profile as he stared at the barn's roof.

"I don't know about that. There was nothing bad about what we just did. If anything, it makes me want to do it again." Her voice even to her own ears sounded sleepy and satisfied. And she was both, wanted nothing but to cuddle up next to him, breathe him in and sleep.

He shut his eyes. "Please forgive me, Lizzie. I should never have done such a thing to you."

The thought of him doing it with anyone else irked her, and she pulled him over to look at her. "I'm not a child, Hugo. I may be inexperienced but I'm not such a naive fool not to know what we did was a normal and pleasurable thing a lot of couples do. Though I know we are not a couple, and I allowed you privileges that are ruinous in the eyes of society. You did not ruin me; there is no risk. So please don't wreck what just happened between us because you think I'm upset or violated in some way, because I'm not."

"I know you're not naive, but I do not want to hurt you." He leaned over and kissed her. "I cannot promise you anything at the moment and therefore I should not have touched one hair on your body."

"And yet, I'm so very glad you did." Lizzie smiled, clasping his jaw and running her hand over the prickly stubble. "You never did tell me what you're going to do when your uncle arrives. Are you going to talk to him about the will?"

"I am," he said, taking her hand and kissing her palm with little pecks. "I will ask him to reconsider taking the funds and instead leave them in the estate, allowing me to therefore marry whomever I choose."

"Do you think he'll agree?" And if he didn't, what did that mean for her? With very few words she could relieve Hugo of all his troubles, especially as it looked as if he wanted her and not Miss Fox. The words hovered on the tip of her tongue that she was an heiress, that if he married her all his financial woes would be moot, but she did not.

To tell Hugo her secret would be breaking a promise to Lord Leighton, her cousin and the man who had enabled her future to be so secure in the first place. He'd made her promise not to let anyone know of her change in fortunes. He wanted to ensure that should she marry, the man would be worthy and in love.

But it was not only because of her cousin that Lizzie remained quiet. Her parents' marriage had not been a happy one, often plagued by frequent arguments and unbidden loathing. If she married Lord Wakely after telling him of her inheritance, how would she ever really know he married her because he loved her and not because he simply desired her more than Miss Fox? His choice was not easy and she wished she could help him, but this was one decision he would have to make on his own.

"That I can't tell you, but by God I hope he does. I couldn't stomach lo—"

Losing you. He didn't need to finish what he was saying for Lizzie to hear the unspoken words.

It was not too much to ask, and if they were meant to be together, she had to be patient and wait, allow Lord Wakely to realize that a life without love was no life at all. One could not buy happiness, and as the author of Sense and Sensibility advised herself, happiness in a pocketbook should not outweigh that of the heart.

CHAPTER

TWELVE

Hugo sat on one side of the desk at J. Smith &
Sons Solicitors, listening as his father's final will
and testament was read out loud to him again.
This time in the presence of his uncle, his only
remaining living relative. Not that the man cared for the
sentiment—he'd been cold from the moment he arrived, and
it didn't bode well for Hugo's strategy.

In appearance, his uncle was the male version of his
mother, and it made Hugo nostalgic for her. Not to mention
she would be appalled that her husband had done this to
their only child. After today, if his uncle did not refuse to
take the inheritance, Hugo would have very little to live on,
or to keep his three estates running. Did his father not think
out his final blow? To be so reckless with the lives of their
tenants and their servants was reprehensible.

Hugo shook his head as the clause ordering him to
marry an heiress was read aloud. He should have married
as soon as he'd heard the will almost a year ago. Had he
done so he wouldn't be sitting here today, on the brink of
losing everything other than his title. His father might have

stipulated for him to marry, but Hugo had wasted the past year with recklessness and endless enjoyment. This was as much his fault as anyone else's.

Mr. Thompson pulled off his pince-nez glasses and placed them on the mahogany table. "Now that you've heard the will and the stipulations, we may proceed."

Hugo's uncle leaned back in his chair, steepling his fingers. "I'm sorry that your father has placed you in this position, Hugo, I really am. But your family across the Atlantic is also in dire need of cash. I thought that you would've married by now and my trip over here wouldn't have been necessary, but I cannot deny that I'm happy you have not. I will be enforcing the clause and claiming the money Elizabeth was given as her dowry upon the marriage to your father."

The blow was like a quick uppercut to the nose. He fought not to cast up his accounts with the realization of what was about to happen. "Uncle, please. There are many who work for my estates, both as servants and tenant farmers, and their families. If you enable my father's clause to stand, if you enforce it, my suffering will be nothing compared to theirs. They will lose everything."

His uncle snipped the end of his cigar off and lit it, taking great puffs of smoke. He shrugged. "And I'm sorry for them, but I must think of my family, and the people who work for me."

"Could you compromise?" Mr. Thompson suggested. "Receive only half the funds so Lord Wakely can continue to run the estates?"

"No," his uncle said, shaking his head. "I'm not willing to compromise. I'm sorry it has come to this, Hugo, but you've had twelve months. Your father wrote to me explaining what he'd done, and while it may not be fair, your lifestyle has been frivolous to say the least. A point proven yet again by the fact that you've had nearly a year to marry and void this clause and you've not done so. Have you even found a woman whom you'd like as your wife? Have you even been looking?"

Hugo leaned back in his chair. He could feel his temper rising and took a couple of deep breaths to calm himself. "I think you're forgetting the clause that I'm only to marry an heiress."

"Are there not plenty of those about town?" His uncle dabbed out his cigar. "I'm sure you could marry some chit who's after a coronet and can offer blunt in return."

The image of Miss Fox came to mind, the very woman who could do exactly that. The thought left Hugo cold. He didn't want Miss Fox. In fact, he didn't want to marry a woman simply because she had money. "Of course there are women about town like that." But he didn't want one of those. Hell, he'd resigned himself to do just that so he could save his tenants and employees—a noble sacrifice—but then he'd gone and kissed Lizzie Doherty, and she'd opened his eyes to how great a sacrifice his actions would be. He wanted to marry a woman who was kind, passionate, and caring. One with whom he could converse and laugh freely, someone with whom he personally melded. He wanted her.

His uncle stood. "I'm sorry, my boy, I know you wanted the meeting today to go a different way, but alas it will not. I'll not change my mind, so I suggest you marry a rich debutante sooner rather than later, for you only have a week left before I claim the money. If you need me for anything, I'm staying at the Grand Hotel in Covent Garden until I sail on the first of the month."

Hugo watched him leave, and all his hopes along with them. "Well, that puts paid to that," he said to Mr. Thompson, meeting his solicitor's gaze and hating the pity he read in his visage.

"I'm sorry, Lord Wakely. I know this wasn't what you wanted to hear."

"No, it wasn't." He rubbed a hand over his jaw. Whatever would he do? However would he manage the estates without sufficient money? Without funds, it would be impossible to maintain the estates and provide a living for the tenants and staff. And with the homes entailed, he wasn't able to sell them. They would, over time, simply rot.

"If I may be so bold as to ask if you've considered an heiress? A wedding can be arranged in under a week if need be. You may best your uncle yet and keep your money while satisfying your father's last request."

"By marrying an heiress, I will lose the woman I do care for. A woman who deserves so much more than what I've given her." He was to meet Lizzie tomorrow, and the thought of telling her the outcome of today's meeting left an unpleasant taste in his mouth. Although they had not spoken of marriage, the affection he felt for her, the hints he'd given to her, would no doubt have alerted her to his wanting more. And now he could give her nothing, for he was ruined. She deserved so much better than him.

Hugo stood, taking his gloves and walking stick from a waiting clerk. "Thank you, Mr. Thompson, for your assistance today. I'll see myself out." He left, and, making the street outside, stood for a moment in the warm afternoon sun. Still, he was chilled. What was he going to do? Could he place Lizzie before all who relied on him for their livelihood? Would she even marry him knowing all that he stood to lose?

He hailed a hackney and called out his address. He needed time to think about it all, to figure out what his best course of action would be. His steward was also arriving today to discuss the financials of his estates. Once that was completed he would know the best way forward, but whether the best way for the estates would also be the best way for him was yet to be seen.

Lizzie sat atop her white mare, quietly watching the other riders on Rotten Row. Some were enjoying a slow canter, while others, like her, were simply sitting, watching, waiting... She spied her groom waiting patiently a little way away from her, and frowned.

Where was he? She looked about the park again but couldn't see Lord Wakely approaching either on foot or horseback. She checked the time once again and her stomach knotted. Lord Wakely had sent a missive to meet him here–had something happened to him? He was over two hours late.

She turned her mare toward the northern gate. She would return home. Maybe there was a missive waiting for her. A reason as to why he hadn't come.

The thought crossed her mind that it had been a deliberate snub, and she shook it aside. She didn't want to think like that. It was neither helpful nor nice, and until she knew for certain, then and only then would she worry about it.

But upon returning home and finding no note, she couldn't help but surmise his meeting with his uncle and the solicitor the day before had not gone well. Which meant Lord Wakely had a decision to make. Marry Miss Fox and her thousands of pounds, a marriage of convenience and little affection, if any. Or, he could marry her, a woman whom he believed to have no dowry, but would love him unconditionally until the day she died. If only he'd prove his worth and choose her.

The thought again crossed her mind that she should tell him she would have enough dowry to satisfy his father's will, and therefore no money from his estate would be lost to his uncle. Hugo did care for her a great deal, and maybe more than she believed. He wouldn't be struggling with his choice if he did not. Maybe she ought to bring it up with her cousin Lord Leighton and seek his counsel. See if he thought it time that Lord Wakely knew the truth, especially in light of him being on the brink of losing his inheritance.

There were so many people reliant on Lord Wakely's estate. In total he would have hundreds of people, with hundreds more counting their families, who needed employment, and who would suffer if they were to lose their positions. Knowing all this, surely Lord Leighton would reconsider his decision on keeping her status as a wealthy woman secret. The last thing Lizzie wanted was to be the cause for so many people suffering when she had the power to stop it.

She thought back to their times together. Other than not turning up today, he'd never done anything that would give her any cause for alarm. He was attentive and trustworthy. Surely knowing she was an heiress wouldn't be the sole reason why he would offer for her. She usually had a good understanding of people's characters, and Lord Wakely's, for all his roguish past, was good-natured and honest.

LATER THAT AFTERNOON LIZZIE SAT BEFORE HER COUSIN LORD Leighton in his library. He idly flicked through some papers and she waited patiently, her mind a whirr of thoughts over how to go about explaining this predicament so that she might change his mind regarding the secrecy about her dowry.

He placed the papers into a folder, then, clasping his hands on his desk, gave her his full attention. "Sorry, Lizzie. I just had to finish that piece of business. Now, what was it you wished to talk with me about?"

Nerves pitted in her stomach and she pushed them aside. Her cousin would see sense, he was a good man. She was sure of it. "I wanted to speak to you about a gentleman whom I believe I would like to consider marrying. And before I tell you who it is, I need you to promise me you'll not get angry with me. He's probably not who you thought I would look toward to be my husband."

Lord Leighton leaned back in his chair, crossing his arms. Lizzie ignored the fact it was a defensive stance and instead steeled herself to remain calm and discuss the situation like the grown adults that they both were.

"Who is this gentleman?" he asked, his voice weary.

"The gentleman is Lord Wakely." At the mention of Hugo's name, Lord Leighton sat bolt upright in his chair, his eyes wide in shock.

"Hugo? You cannot possibly be serious. What on earth makes you believe he's even looking for a wife? He's not exactly the most settled gentleman in London. If anything, he's quite the rogue."

"I know all about his past. You've been friends with him for years, and I'm not blind. But he is looking for a wife, and I believe should he know of my financial situation he would offer for me."

"You mean he would marry you if he knew you were rich. Absolutely not." His words brooked no argument and Lizzie took a calming breath.

"Listen, there is more to the story than that. Let me explain."

"Well, I certainly hope you will, for as it stands right now my answer is not to agree to whatever you're going to ask me."

Lizzie threw him a quelling look and continued. "The reason his uncle is here is because of his father's will. His sire had included a clause in his will that Lord Wakely was to marry within twelve months of his death, and also to an heiress of no less than thirty thousand pounds. If he does not, his mother's dowry money will revert to her American family. But you see," she continued, "he's been courting me, believing I have no dowry, and now he's conflicted. I could remove that conflict from his life. If I told him of my fortune, he would not be struggling with his choice, for I believe he would choose me."

"Over Miss Fox I gather, if the talk through the *ton* is any indication."

Lizzie nodded. "Yes, that's right. Lord Wakely has so many people relying on him, so many staff and dependents. If he were to lose his inheritance, then with what would he run the estates? If he married me he would adhere to the clause, and therefore no money would be lost. I want to tell him, Hamish. Will you give me permission?"

Lord Leighton rubbed his jaw while he thought about her request. "As much as I would like to say yes, Lizzie, I cannot. I know Lord Wakely, very well, and if he really wanted to marry you he would find another way in which to raise the money required to run his estates. Surely marrying an heiress is not his only option."

Lizzie frowned, wondering if he had considered other ways. "Even if there was another way, he's left it a little late now. He's to marry before the end of the month. And if he's not married, he loses that money. I could stop that."

"But why should you be his saviour? He's in this situation because of the way he lived his life, something he knew his father loathed. As much as I care for Lord Wakely, and would help him if I could, I cannot allow you to be the reason he remains one of the richest men in England. Lord Wakely should have other means of income—investments, art, anything that is not entailed that would help him marry whomever he wanted."

Lizzie bit back the tears that threatened as her future with Lord Wakely vanished before her eyes. She sniffed and Hamish shifted in his chair.

"I'll tell you what, I shall speak to him, see what we can figure out. Maybe he's not tried any other options, or not thought of them. I want a good marriage for you, my dear. I've seen too many unions within the *ton* that are toxic and barely civilized. Your parents' marriage was one of them, as if I need remind you. Katherine and I love you, and want the man who marries you to love you unconditionally, not because of how much money they gain from the union."

Lizzie pulled out her handkerchief and dabbed at her nose. "Just because Lord Wakely would marry me because I had a fortune, does not mean that he does not care for me. Love me even. He's responsible for so many. The choice would not be easy. I would think should you have been in the same situation with Katherine, you would've faltered too. I know how much you care for your tenant farmers, your staff. Can you honestly tell me that you would not marry for money to keep all of that side of your life safe?"

He cringed, meeting her gaze. "You forget I married a woman who wasn't my social equal. I broke all the rules to have Katherine by my side and I would do it all again. But as a business owner with estates such as I and Lord Wakely have, these are businesses, they are homes entrusted into our care for the next generation. I expected to run those properties, put into place secure investments, and have the best stewards around so I never needed to marry an heiress to keep it all safe. Lord Wakely has not done that, and now he is paying the price. You said he's had twelve months. Pray tell me, what has he done in that time to shore up his homes so that he could lose the money and still marry you?"

Lizzie stared at her cousin, her mind conflicted over what to do. "I do not think he's done anything, my lord." All hope fled, and she didn't think she could feel any more dejected than she did right at that moment.

"Neither do I." Lord Leighton stood and came around the desk, pulling her to stand. "I promised you six years ago that I would ensure you married a man who would love and cherish you always. I will speak to Lord Wakely and see if he's worthy of you. Maybe he does have other plans you're not privy to. If he does, I'll give you my consent. If not, then I'm sorry Lizzie, but I cannot give you away to such a life. I will not release your inheritance simply to line an impoverished man's pockets."

CHAPTER
THIRTEEN

Later that night Lizzie ordered a bath and then declined going out with Lord Leighton and Katherine, who were attending a private dinner. She dismissed her maid for the night, wanting to soak in the bath and plan. How could she show Lord Wakely that they were perfect for one another?

After her conversation this afternoon with her cousin, all hope of a life with Hugo seemed to have disappeared. But that did not mean she could not try one last time to have him offer for her, penniless as he thought she was. She couldn't tell him the truth, Lord Leighton had not allowed that, but perhaps if he was with her again, he would tell her of his plans to secure his estates and those who relied on him that didn't include an heiress.

Her fingers tapped the side of the bath and, knowing what she would do, she stood and dried herself quickly. She dressed in a simple gown with buttons at the front, one she could manage without a maid, and pulled on the darkest cloak she owned.

Opening her bedroom door, she checked for servants,

and seeing none, scuttled across the hall to the stairs, stopping again to check who was about. Hearing no one and assuming that the staff were eating their supper, she went down the stairs and started for the back of the house. The back parlor had doors that led out into the yard and a side gate that she could use to slip out.

It didn't take very long to reach Lord Wakely's house, as he lived within a couple of blocks, and in this part of London, with many couples out walking just as she was, Lizzie felt reasonably safe. Just like her cousin's home, Lord Wakely had a side alley that one could access the backyard through. Coming to the wooden gate, she checked her surroundings then pushed it open, closing it quickly behind her.

The house was dark apart from a couple of lamps burning in the upstairs rooms. Movement behind a door that led out onto a small balcony and the silhouette which Lizzie would recognize anywhere told her it was his lordship.

She pursed her lips, surveying the home. There was no way she could climb up to his floor from the outside, so she had to find a way to sneak in from below. Pulling her cloak tighter about her neck and ensuring the cape covered her hair, she inched her way across the garden and toward the back door, of which there were two. One led into the kitchens, if the sound of clanging pots and loud chatter was any indication. Lizzie took her chances on the other door, and sagged in relief when she turned the handle and found it unlocked.

Stepping into a darkened passage, a door slammed somewhere close by. She froze as panic seized her that she would be caught. The sound was followed by silence, no hurried footsteps or staff talking amongst themselves, so she continued on.

Walking quickly through the hall, she came to the servant's stairs and ran up them toward the first floor. Exiting through a door, she came to a shadowy, sparsely lit hall. She tried to gauge her whereabouts, based on when she'd looked at the house from the outside.

It was not easy as most of the rooms' doors were closed, bar one that was slightly ajar and had the faintest flicker of candlelight peeking out. She took a chance and tiptoed up to the door, her stomach in knots over what she was about to do, what she was about to offer Lord Wakely.

Would he send her away? Would he take her in his arms and tell her his absence today was a mistake? She wasn't sure how his reaction would play out. Reaching the door, she peeked through the gap to see his lordship shirtless, clad only in tan breeches. He was sitting at the end of his bed, flipping through a document of some sort. He was completely lost in his own thoughts, the frown lines between his brows indicating that whatever he was reading was complicated or troubling. Her need to go to him doubled. She'd never seen him look so wretched, and if she could she'd put a stop to it tonight.

She entered the room and shut the door quickly, the snip of the lock loud in the otherwise quiet space. The shock on Hugo's face was comical and her lips twitched.

"What are you doing here?" he asked, the papers in his hands dropping to his feet as he stood.

Lizzie swallowed, fighting to bring forth all the determination she'd felt coming over here. Tonight she would have Lord Wakely if he'd allow, and with any luck he would realize that what they had between them wasn't like anything he'd encountered before. It was so for Lizzie at least, and she was willing to risk her reputation to be with Hugo if it meant that she could win him.

Never before had she wanted anything as much as she wanted the man who stood before her, his mouth agape, his chest rising and lowering rapidly with every breath. Should she not win his heart, it was not for want of trying, and she wouldn't win another's after tonight. If Lord Wakely turned her away, she would wait out her time, accept her fortune, and leave London. Travel the world, go to Italy and buy an olive farm, and adopt stray cats just because she could.

"You didn't arrive at our ride today. I was worried."

He cringed. "I'm sorry, Lizzie. The meeting with my solicitor didn't go well and I forgot. Do you forgive me?"

She strode over to him and pushed him back onto the bed. He bounced, his eyes widening in surprise. She took charge and, steeling her back, climbed onto the bed and straddled his waist. "There is nothing to forgive. And as for what I'm really doing here, well," she said, sliding her hands over his muscular shoulders and enjoying the feel of his skin beneath her palms, "I'm seducing you, my lord."

If she thought she'd shocked him before it was nothing to how he looked now. Totally flabbergasted and without words he stared up at her, before his face darkened in hunger and he flipped her over, pinning her to the bed.

She squealed, having not expected the move, and her stomach clenched in delicious tremors. Ever since their first kiss she'd dreamed of being with him so. Of touching him, kissing him, without the threat of interruption.

"You have no idea how much I've wanted you beneath me, just as you are now." He bent down and kissed her, a sweet, soft melding of lips that left her following him as he pulled away. Wanting more of the same, not less. Never less. "Before we go any further, tell me why you're here. I need to hear it."

Lizzie shivered at the deep, tightly harnessed need she heard in his voice. She wanted to break that control, see what he was like in his full, wild glory.

"I'm here because I want to be with you. I want you to make love to me." *Love me as I love you.* Heat bloomed on her cheeks and she bit her lip, hoping he wouldn't push her away. That she hadn't been wrong in what she knew to be between them.

He leaned back, running his finger over her cloak, untying it from her neck and pushing it aside to lay about her like a halo. "I shouldn't allow this. You're a maid. I'd be the worst rogue to walk the earth to have you like this."

Lizzie studied him a moment, waiting to see what he would choose. It had to be his choice. She would not beg.

He frowned, shutting his eyes. "Damn it, Lizzie, but I cannot stay away." He slid one hand down her legs and clasped the hem of her gown, pushing it up to bunch at her waist. "I want you naked beneath me. I want to see all that you are. I will, however," he said, throwing her a mischievous grin, "allow your silk stockings to remain."

Heat pooled at her core and she writhed, needing him to touch her. "How very naughty of you, my lord."

"Hugo, please. No titles between us. Not ever again."

Lizzie was only too willing to do as he asked, and in a flurry of movement he had divested them both of their garments. The clothes lay pooled about the bed, and Lizzie chuckled as he came back over her, his hair askew, his eyes bright with expectation.

She fought to control her body, that no longer felt like her own. The touches he bestowed as he stripped her naked left her aching, and not for the first time she clenched her thighs if only to give herself a little relief.

The hair on his chest tickled, the skin on his back was warm and smooth, and he had the most intoxicating smell of sandalwood and something else that was solely Hugo. He kissed her deeply, seducing her with his mouth, and she gave way to the sensations, the want she had for him.

So this was why her cousin's wife always looked at her husband with such love and reverence. Why their marriage was a loving and obviously passionate one. Hugo lowered his head to her breast, taking one nipple between his lips before licking it with sweet teasing. She moaned, her fingers spiking into his hair to hold him against her. "That's wicked, Hugo."

He blew on her nipple and it puckered at the chill, before he licked it once again. "I want you so much it hurts. From the first moment I saw you enter Lady X's parlor I knew I had to have you. That I wanted you and would never allow another to touch one hair on your pretty head." He placed a soft kiss against her lips. "But are you sure, Lizzie? There is no coming back from this action should we proceed. You will no longer be a maid."

She cupped his cheek, the prickling of his stubble rough against her palm. "I no longer care about being a maid. I've wanted this too for so long, much longer than you'll ever know, and there is nothing in the world that will stop me from what we're about to do."

"You've wanted me for some time?" He rocked against her core, spiking need throughout her body.

"Oh, yes," she gasped, not entirely in reply to his question but also due to his actions. "I noticed you long before you ever noticed me."

"Hmm, you may be wrong about that."

She ran her hand against the nape of his neck and pulled him down to her. "Really? Tell me then."

He stared at her a moment before a mischievous smile tweaked his lips. "The only reason I did not act before now was due to my friendship with Lord Leighton. Of all the people in the *ton*, he knows of my past, my indiscretions. I knew he would not look favourably on my courting of you. But when I saw you at Lady X's, all bets were off."

Lizzie lifted her leg to sit up against his hip. The action brought him closer to her and desire ran hot through his gaze. Warmth pooled at her core and she longed for him to continue what they'd started. "They like you, in spite of your rakish tendencies."

A muscle worked in his jaw and he stared at her a moment. "Lord Leighton will never forgive me for what we're about to do."

"He'll never know," she said, sliding her hands down his back to clasp his buttocks. She pulled him against her, helping to dispense some of her need.

He swore, sucking in a startled breath. "True," he managed.

And with those words he settled against her fully, and with painful care guided himself into her. The sensation was odd, but not wholly unpleasant. Her mother had spoken of searing pain, and tedious annoyance until one ripened with a child. But this, this right now with Hugo, was anything but tedious, anything but painful.

It was delightful.

Taking a deep breath, Lizzie tried to relax and understand the fullness, the sensations that were swarming through her body. Hugo did not rush her. With perfect care, he allowed her to get used to his size before pulling out a little, only to then thrust back within her.

The dance made her crave him even more, and she soon found herself moving with him. He kissed her throughout and she gasped when pleasure thrummed at her core.

"I do not want to hurt you, Lizzie." His voice sounded strained and she shook her head, words eluding her for a moment.

"You're not hurting me." She kissed him deep and long, sliding her tongue against his, the kaleidoscope of feelings he brought forth almost too much to contain. "Keep going. Don't ever stop."

He pushed deeper, and she moaned, her body breathless, a light sheen of sweat chilling her skin. His actions became frantic, harder, more demanding, and yet something was missing. It was like a peak was out of her reach, teasing her close by before floating away.

"I feel...I want...oh dear, I do not know what I want," she gasped as he continued his onslaught of her emotions.

He leaned down, kissing her ear. "You desire pleasure. Not that you know what that is yet, but I'm about to show you." He slid his hand between them and touched her mons. With each thrust he flicked across her flesh. He owned her. At this very time Lizzie would allow him to do anything he pleased if only he would never stop.

What was he doing to her? This love making was more intense, the sensations more vivid than when they were together at Lady X's. It was as if she could shatter into a million pieces and still remain whole. With one last flick, he thrust into her hard, and the peak she had climbed but never assailed crested. She tumbled into unimaginable pleasure, calling out his name as wave after wave flowed through her.

There were no words for the delectable tremors and pulsating thrums that overtook her body. Hugo gasped out her name, kissing her as his thrusts, hard and constant, battered her body. But before his release, he pulled out, stroking himself above her belly. Lizzie watched enthralled as he found his release outside of her, and she couldn't stop herself from reaching out and touching him, sliding her hand about his shaft and helping him find his pleasure.

Their eyes met and held, and with his look Lizzie tumbled over into love with him. There would never be anyone else but Hugo for her. They were simply meant to be.

He flopped beside her, then, reaching over to the bedside cabinet, he grabbed a discarded cravat and wiped her belly clean. "I do apologize, it can be a messy business."

She didn't care about any of that. All she cared about was when they would meet next. Hugo seemed to be thinking the same.

"When can I see you again? I do not think I can go a day without being near you," he stated, throwing the cravat onto the floor.

Lizzie rolled over and snuggled against his chest. His arm circled her shoulder and kept her close. "I'm attending the Ramsays' masquerade two nights from now. I'm dressing as Queen Elizabeth with a blue satin mask if you wish to seek me out."

"I will find you."

Her heart warmed at his words, and as the clock chimed the late hour she sighed, sitting up. "I need to go before I'm missed. Will you help me dress?"

He slid his hand over her bare back, following the line of her spine and making her shiver. "I would like you to stay."

Lizzie turned to look at him and grinned. "I think we both know that cannot happen, but we'll meet again. In two days in fact, and I shall reserve the first waltz if you wish."

Hugo sat up, pushing her hair over her shoulder to pool across her breast before kissing her nape. "I should not miss it for the world."

CHAPTER

FOURTEEN

I f Lord Wakely was a rogue, Lizzie most definitely was fast. She grinned and continued her stroll through Hyde Park, her maid a short distance behind her immersed in a booklet about the different plant species found in England. Lizzie looked up between the green leaves of the trees, and breathed deep the fresh air and warm dappled sunlight. From the moment she'd left Hugo's bed the other night, the world had seemed brighter somehow, more alive and vivid.

And she was a fallen woman, well and truly, and for some illogical reason she was pleased by the knowledge. Maybe because after what they shared they were a little more even in their knowledge. The fact that she'd seduced *him* in the end too had taken the choice out of his lordship's hands. Seizing what she wanted had brought pride to her soul. Never before had she been so bold or determined, and now that she'd lain with Hugo she wanted nothing more than to do it again.

Be damned the consequences.

"Good afternoon, Miss Doherty. How providential to run into you here at the park."

Butterflies took flight in her stomach and she clasped her abdomen to calm her nerves. "Lord Wakely," she said, dipping into a curtsy. "It is lovely to see you again."

Although they would see each other this evening at the masked ball, the last two days had been endless. Lizzie had debated seeking his lordship out once more, but in the end decided against it. Even if they were lovers, she didn't wish him to think she was so desperate for his touch that she couldn't wait thirty-six hours. She needed him to want her as much as she wanted him. He was the one who needed to fall in love with her, ask for her hand in marriage, and somehow come up with a plan that would solve his money troubles without having to marry an heiress.

"Are you looking forward to the ball tonight, my lord?" A wicked gleam entered the viscount's eyes and Lizzie chuckled.

"I am. *Very* much so." They walked on and the answering smile from Hugo told Lizzie he understood her meaning. She leaned toward him to ensure privacy. "Where shall we meet?"

His eyes warmed with appreciation and desire. He placed her hand atop his arm and continued to stroll. "Sir Ramsay's home has two servant staircases. Use the one closest to the ballroom. If you go into the entrance hall, under the guise of using the retiring room, and turn toward the back of the house, the staircase is to your right. I will wait for you on the stairs."

"And then what?" Lizzie met Hugo's eyes, and the heat she read in them left her in no doubt as to what they would do after that. Although she would like to hear it nevertheless.

"I shall lead you up to one of the guest bedrooms, where I shall strip every article of clothing from your person. I shall kiss every inch of your body and bring you to pleasure using nothing but my mouth," he whispered against her ear, the breath of his words making her shiver.

Heat suffused her cheeks, but she dismissed her embarrassment, too enthralled with the thought of what he was going to do. What could he possibly mean? She thought on his words a moment and couldn't figure out what it meant, but even so, it would prove to be a delicious night if he made her feel anything like she did two nights ago.

"Is what you're saying even possible?" She had to know, wanted a visual to look forward to until they met this evening. And Lord Wakely could kiss very well, his mouth was most talented, so he probably could do what he promised if he remained determined.

"You shall be pleasantly surprised by what my mouth can do with the help of my tongue."

Oh, my...

"And in return you shall pleasure me with yours if you like."

Lizzie shut her mouth with a snap as a myriad of thoughts entered her mind. And if her thoughts were correct, well, how scandalous. How cocooned she'd lived, having no idea that couples even did such a thing.

She checked to see the location of her maid, sighing in relief when she found her engrossed in her book and a safe distance away from them. "How is that even possible?" she whispered, intrigued.

"Think on it and tonight you can tell me if you figured it out." Hugo stepped back and bowed. "Until this evening, Miss Doherty."

Lizzie curtsied. "Good day, Lord Wakely." She watched

him walk away, annoyed a little at his refusal to tell her what she wanted to know. He looked back at her and grinned over his shoulder, and excitement thrummed through her blood. Tonight couldn't come soon enough. Turning about, she summoned her maid to return home. She needed to take a bath and get ready. And maybe sneak down to the library and try to find out for herself what Hugo meant about the pleasure a woman could give a man using her mouth. There had to be something to explain his cryptic taunt.

By the time Hugo arrived, the ball was in full swing and the room was full to capacity. The hundreds of wax candles above the ballroom floor were surrounded by a smoke haze thanks to the men who were enjoying their cigars and cheroots, discussing politics or horses while watching the dancers and society at play.

Being sociable wasn't on Hugo's mind this evening, but having Lizzie again was. It was all he'd thought about the last two days. After seeing her this afternoon he was without doubt that he cared for her more than anyone ever in his life. He longed to talk with her, to walk as they had in the park, to confide and trust in her, not just have her warm his bed.

But as to actually marrying her, he was still undecided. So much hung on his decision. He now had only days left before he would lose his mother's fortune, leaving him with little to run the estates. Miss Fox strode past him, her black silk gown and mask suiting her dark nature. She nodded her head in greeting and he bowed, watching her. If he married Miss Fox all his troubles would be over. He would keep his fortune, and his estates would be safe. But Lizzie would be lost to him. He ran a hand over his jaw. There had to be another way to keep his estates afloat. But how?

Never in his life had he hated his father as much as he hated him now.

He spied his quarry in a sapphire gown, the blue of her mask bringing out the color of her eyes. The large ornate collar and her red hair made it easy to figure out he'd found his queen. She stood beside her mother, who had obviously decided not to wear a costume. The small upturn of Lizzie's lips told him she'd spied him as well, and warmth spread through his blood. Without delay he headed in her direction.

He bowed before them. "Good evening, Mrs. Doherty, Miss Doherty," he said. "I wonder, Miss Doherty, if you would care to dance. I believe the next set is to be a waltz."

"I would love to dance, thank you, Lord Wakely." Lizzie took his arm, not giving her mother any consideration as he led her out onto the floor. He twirled her into his arms just as the music started, she laughed at being handled so.

Lizzie was the most delightful creature he'd ever met, carefree and honest. Panic seized him at the thought that he adored her and yet might not be able to keep her for himself. Not if he couldn't find a solution to his problem.

She fitted him so perfectly, in so many ways, that he couldn't help but wonder why it was that he'd never really seen her before. Before his father had passed. Had he done so, had his sire seen him marry, he would never have punished him with the clause in the will that now stood. He would've been happy for Hugo, happy the title had a future and the possibility of heirs. In all truth, the reason he was in this predicament was solely due to his own selfishness and refusal to grow up.

"Has anyone ever told you, Lord Wakely, that you dance divinely?"

He maneuvered them around other couples with expert ease. "They may have, but yours is the first opinion that I've cared to hear."

"You flatter me, my lord." She smiled up at him. Something in his chest ached and he couldn't help but grin back at the little minx.

"I do flatter you because you deserve to be flattered. Tonight, tomorrow, and all the days that follow." Her startled expression caught him unawares, possibly as unaware as his own words. Next he'd be quoting poetry and writing love sonnets to her. The idea didn't wholly disgust him, and that in itself was telling.

Shit, he cared for Lizzie, more than he'd ever cared for anyone. The overwhelming need to know that she was well, happy, and safe overrode all his other concerns, even those regarding his estates and tenants. How would he ever give her up simply so he could keep his fortune?

"You should not say such things, or I'll start to think you're a romantic like Lord Byron."

He pulled her closer than he ought, fighting the urge to wrench her hard against his chest and never let her go. "Not ever will I be as bad as Lord Byron."

Lizzie moved perfectly in tune with him, and the feel of her silk gown sliding beneath his hand reminded him of their night of passion. Her gloved hand on his shoulder tightened a little and he met her gaze, wishing he could drown in her deep blue eyes.

"Shall we agree that after the next set we shall reacquaint ourselves in the location discussed?" she said, her eyes bright with mischief.

Hugo cleared his throat as lust roared through him. "I...yes."

She all but purred in his arms, and the knowledge that within the hour they would be pleasuring each other made the short sixty minutes seem too far away. He slowed them as they turned at the bottom of the ballroom floor, before making their way up along the other side. "I don't believe I've told you how very beautiful you look this evening."

"You just did." Lizzie laughed, a throaty, seductive sound that made him harden in an instant.

"Before I have the urge to place you on my shoulders and carry you out of here like a caveman, tell me what you've been doing the last two days, other than the time we met in the park of course. I'm hoping you've been a little more productive than myself. I have struggled to have coherent thoughts since you left my bedroom."

"Is this your way of telling me that you've missed me, my lord? You do know that for a man of your reputation, you're putting it in danger by saying such things. Anyone would think that you longed to see me again. That you cared."

How true that was. Lizzie was the only thing that had occupied his mind for the past two days. In fact, before he espied her in the park he'd even considered sending for his stable staff to prepare two horses, so they could go riding. It was only luck that he'd come by her in Hyde Park.

He watched her as they danced and the thought of her being married to some other gentleman made his guts clench. She would never do for anyone else, since she fitted him so perfectly. And yet, while he wished she could be his, if he made it so, he would lose everything. His tenants would lose everything.

He scoffed and pulled them into a tight turn, knowing

how unfair and selfish he was being. To give hope where there was none was not something he should do, and yet he could not help himself. He didn't want to give her up. Didn't want to be in this position.

"What are you scowling at, my lord? You seem very fierce at the moment."

Hugo shook his thoughts aside and made himself more congenial. "Tell me more about you. I want to know everything."

She sighed, possibly in relief, and threw herself into the new topic. "Well," she said, frowning a little in thought, "I enjoy horses and riding more so than I like being out in society. That was always Mama's idea, and her desire to find me a good husband. I hate seafood but love sweets. I enjoy shopping, and going to horse races. As you know, I want to travel to Italy one day, possibly even live there for a time."

"I have been to Rome. It's a wonderful city, full of history, and the streets smell of olives and herbs."

She chuckled. "It doesn't smell like that, you made that up."

He laughed. "I did, it doesn't smell the best, but it is old. Ancient, in fact. You will love it when you get there, which I have no doubt you will accomplish one day."

"What else can you tell me about it? I'd love to know."

For the remainder of the dance Hugo told Lizzie about his entire trip abroad and the wonderful people he had met along the way. He spoke of the ruins of the Circus Maximus, the Colosseum and the gladiatorial bouts that had occurred there, how unbelievably majestic it must have been to see it during its glory days. Of the beautiful villas, and the bath-houses, some of which still ran today. As they talked, their discussion turned to other subjects, that of books and what authors they enjoyed, including one in particular that they did not agree about.

"She's not at all writing a sensible story. I highly doubt the Bennett sisters would've found such high and well-connected marriages in real life."

"I'm not titled, although I do have a gentleman father, may he rest in peace, and a cousin who's titled, and yet here I am, talking to a viscount. And," she added, looking about them, "from the annoyed glances I'm getting from some of the ladies present, I can only assume they're put out with me taking up so much of an eligible man's time."

"You deserve my whole attention." It took all of Hugo's control not to lean down and kiss her. Warmth spread through his chest and he could barely wait to have her alone.

Everything that Lizzie and he had spoken of was intelligent and noteworthy. They had not agreed on everything, and she did not shy away from telling him her opinion, or when she thought his was misplaced.

Hugo had never been able to stomach the idea of a wife who had no independent thought. He doubted that Miss Fox would even care about his opinion or giving hers. Her interest in him had never been anything other than an alliance—a contract.

In the weeks since they'd returned from Lady X's house party, Lizzie had become a woman who demanded his respect and admiration. The dance came to an end and, taking her hand and placing it on his arm, he started back toward her mama. "It's eleven o'clock. In fifteen minutes, meet me in the stairway as planned."

She nodded but didn't reply, simply curtsied and rejoined her parent. Hugo lingered for a couple of minutes before heading toward where they would rendezvous.

Excitement thrummed through his blood at having her to himself, alone and away from the *ton*'s prying eyes. Very, very alone, where they could get to know each other a little more, but in the biblical sense.

LIZZIE SLOWLY WANDERED OVER TOWARD THE BALLROOM DOORS, and when she was certain no one was watching what she was doing, she exited the room, walking quickly toward the servant's stairs where Hugo said he would be waiting.

Finding the door that was made to look like the wall, she pushed it open and slipped away, shutting it quickly and standing there a moment to adjust her vision to the darkened space.

She stifled a scream when he stepped out of the shadows and wrapped his arm about her waist, taking the opportunity to kiss her softly. Lizzie threw herself against him, her body tight and longing for more. It seemed like weeks since she'd been with him intimately, not only a couple of days. The man was addictive and she was sorely suffering cravings when not around him.

"Where to from here?" she whispered when he finally broke away.

He pulled her toward the stairs. "Follow me." They travelled up two flights of stairs before Hugo peeked out into the hall and, seeing it clear of anyone else, pulled her into a room across the way and locked the door.

It was a guest chamber, clean but sparsely furnished. An emerald duvet sat on the bed, and the curtains of the same color hung across the two windows that faced the square. There was a chaise lounge before the unlit fireplace.

"Come here," Hugo said, his voice deep, his eyes warm and inviting.

Lizzie's body didn't feel like her own and she all but thrummed with pent-up excitement as she walked over to him and wrapped her arms about his neck. "What do you plan on doing with me, Lord Wakely?" she asked, although she had a fair idea just what he was going to do with her, and she couldn't wait for the pleasure of it.

"I want you to lie on the bed and lift up that beautiful gown so I may kiss you to climax."

Oh my... Without delay, Lizzie did as he bade. Her gown was heavy but with Hugo's help she soon had it ruffled up about her waist. The cool night air kissed her skin and she shivered. He kneeled, then placed his large hands on either side of her legs and pushed outwards, his eyes dark with need and admiration.

Never had she been so exposed, so vulnerable, but even so, she trusted him, knew he would never do anything that she did not want.

He pulled her toward him, placing her mons right before his mouth.

"You're so beautiful," he said, running his finger over her flesh, paying homage to her nubbin that she now knew existed after their previous encounters, and knew just how pleasurable that part of her body could be.

"Stop teasing me, my lord. I cannot bear another second." If he did not touch her soon she would expire. And then his hot breath moved up her thigh with slow tenderness before his lips kissed her *there*...

Lizzie sucked in a breath, unsure as to what she was feeling having him do what he was. The sensation was odd, but when he flicked her with his tongue she couldn't halt the moan that slipped free.

Heat spread across her cheeks and she closed her eyes and allowed herself to just enjoy, forget the embarrassment at being so open to him, under his complete control, and simply give in to what his fabulously clever mouth could do.

Her hands speared into his hair, and she found herself undulating under his touch. How would she ever live without such tactile contact with a man after experiencing such rich pleasures? The thought of Lord Wakely doing this to another woman left her emotionally spent and she pushed the vision away. He was hers, she was sure of it. Such passion and joy was surely uncommon, only happened between couples who cared for each other deeply.

His pace, his ardent response between her legs increased and she shut her eyes, reveling in his touch. "Hugo," she gasped as he slid one long, strong finger into her heat. The sensation of his touch and his tongue was too much and she shattered in his arms, allowing the pleasure to rock through her over and over again as he kissed and drew every last ounce out of her body.

He came over her, his gaze serious. Laying beneath him, Lizzie's bones resembled jelly and she wanted nothing more than to sleep, to curl up in his arms and be with him like this forever.

She reached up and traced his lips with her finger. "Such a wicked man with such a clever mouth."

He flopped beside her, leaning up on one elbow. The sound of voices carried to them from the passage outside and Lizzie stilled. Hugo sat up, pulling her skirts down quickly and fixing his cravat.

"I saw Lizzie went this way, Mrs. Doherty. If you'll follow me."

Lizzie met Hugo's eyes, all traces of pleasure gone.

"That was Lady Leighton and your mother. You must return to the ball and say you stepped outside onto the terrace for air. Tell them you were feeling unwell and needed some time away from the crush of the ball."

Lizzie nodded, standing and fixing her gown some more before checking her hair was back in place. "I'm sorry I couldn't... In any case, goodnight, Hugo."

He pulled her to a stop when she stepped toward the door, and cupping her cheek he kissed her. "Goodnight, Lizzie. We will meet again."

She nodded and slipped away, returning to the ball the way she'd escaped it. Oh yes, she would see him again. Again and again, if only he would choose her.

CHAPTER

FIFTEEN

Hugo sat at his desk and glared at Lord Leighton, one of his oldest and closest friends. But after today that was in doubt, and especially after what he had just said. Hugo would be lucky if the man didn't pummel him to a pulp.

"Katherine saw you, and had it not been for her quick thinking Lizzie's mother would've entered that room and seen who knows what. How dare you disobey me after I told you to stay the hell away from my cousin!"

Hugo had never seen Hamish so angry, and should he find himself in Lord Leighton's situation he could understand his temper. However, Hugo could not help what he'd come to feel for Lizzie. He could no sooner stay away from her than the sea could stay away from the sea bed. It was impossible.

"Do you love her?" Hamish asked him, his eyes as hard as his tone.

Hugo shifted on his chair, having not thought whether what he felt for Lizzie was love. He certainly cared for her a great deal, wanted only the best for her, but love? That he couldn't say. "I don't know what I feel for her, but what I do know is that I have a decision to make, one that is not easy. I care for Lizzie, more than I thought I could care about anyone in the world, but I don't believe it's love." The words spoken aloud rang an alarm in his mind and he frowned. Denying the emotion seemed wrong, didn't sit well with him, and his stomach turned.

"Then tonight at our ball you will announce your betrothal to Miss Fox. She will be in attendance and it would be the perfect location to tell the *ton*. Lizzie no doubt will be upset, but at least she may retire to her rooms, away from prying eyes and gossiping tongues."

"I will not do that to her so publicly. How could you ask such a thing of me? Do you not care for your cousin at all?"

The fury on Hamish's visage gave Hugo pause and he wondered if he'd pushed the earl too far. "I love my cousin, and care for her a great deal, have cared for her for the past six years. Had you not been a blind fool you might have seen her pining after you all these years, but you were too busy dipping your wick about town and now it's too late. You told me yourself of the financial predicament you find yourself in." The earl paused, taking a calming breath. "You had twelve months to look into other options to secure your estate. Such actions might have given you the ability to marry anyone you wished and whenever you wanted. Tell me, what have you been doing with your time, Hugo? Because to me it looks like you've been a sloppy viscount."

"I've been a fool, I know that now. I should have done more than to decide to marry an heiress to solve my problems. But I never banked on Lizzie being as wonderful as she is. To have her I must lose everything, and yet I find myself not wanting to make the decision either."

"Lizzie cannot help you with your financial difficulties,

therefore you need to choose. You either offer for Miss Fox and her thousands of pounds or you offer for my cousin. But I will not allow you to tamper with her emotions any longer. She deserves a man to pick her, to love her for who she is. Are you that man, Hugo? Are you willing to risk all that you have, to have her in your life?"

Hugo swallowed, unsure what he wanted. Oh, who was he kidding? He wanted Lizzie, in all the ways a man wants a woman, and a husband wants a wife. But by doing so his tenants and the servants at his country estates would be unemployed overnight. Their livelihoods gone without notice. He could not do that either. Hamish had said he'd been a sloppy viscount. Well, at least there he might be able to make amends for his wrongs.

Lizzie deserved more than what he could give her. He could give her affection, passion, but little else. They would be forced to live in London, with no country estates, no house parties, and their living would be frugal—the servants in town would have to be minimal. He could not do that to her. She deserved to be lavished with beautiful things, treated and pampered like the goddess she was.

"I will tell her I cannot marry her."

Disappointment crossed Hamish's face and Hugo looked away, not wanting to see reflected in his friend's eyes the dissatisfaction that he himself felt. "No, you will not. You will write a letter right now and I shall deliver it to her. If I know my cousin, and I do, very well, she will try and persuade you otherwise should you not offer for her. I cannot allow her to do that. The man who marries her, if she ever marries, will be worthy. You, Lord Wakely, are not."

Hugo nodded. There was no point in trying to dissuade the earl. He pulled out a piece of parchment and scribbled as best he could a note to Lizzie. A note that he knew would break her heart when she read it. He signed it then folded it and sealed it with wax. "Tell her I'm sorry."

Hamish snatched the note out of his hand and strode to the door. "On reflection, you're disinvited to the ball this evening. I do believe it will be many years before we'll be friends again. Good day."

Hugo stared at the door for some time after it slammed closed. What had he done? His guts churned with the knowledge that Lizzie would read his note, be crushed by his words. He stood and poured himself a brandy. He was a bastard. She would never forgive him. She would never be with him again, and rightfully so.

How was he ever to survive it? That he didn't know, and right at this moment in time he wished he would not. Death was better than this wretched, self-loathing emotion he now had coursing through *h*is blood. The *ton* had always thought him a cad, and now he'd truly earned that name. For the first time in his life, it was true.

LIZZIE SAT IN THE COACH AS IT RUMBLED TOWARD LORD WAKELY'S home. After reading his missive, she'd scrunched it up and thrown it in the fire. If he was going to break her heart, he could damn well look her in the eye and do it. Not hide behind a letter and have her cousin deliver it for him.

The coach rocked to a halt and she jumped out, not waiting for the driver. Without knocking, she opened the front door and let herself in. The butler, on his way to meet the viscount's guest, started at her intrusion and mumbled something about her not disturbing the viscount as he wasn't receiving guests, but she pushed the library door open and slammed it in his face without care.

"What the hell do you think you're doing, Hugo? You think you can write me a letter and I'll just scuttle away like a good little girl?"

His eyes wide, he looked up from the chair before the fire and Lizzie could tell from his bloodshot eyes that he'd hit the brandy. "Lizzie. I—"

"Don't you Lizzie me. How dare you treat me with so little respect. I think after everything we've done, all that I thought we felt for one another, I deserve more than just a note." She took a calming breath, not wanting to lose control of her emotions, although that may happen anyway as her eyes already stung with the threat of tears.

"Your cousin wouldn't allow me to see you."

"You have no right to blame Hamish. He has nothing to do with this. You could've said no to that. You could've said you wanted to speak to me. Explain why you would sleep with a woman, open your heart to her, only to discard her without a backward glance."

Hugo stood, coming over to her. He went to take her hands and she slapped him, hard. He reeled and she swallowed, the sting of her palm nothing to the sting of tears in her eyes. "I loved you." She shook her head, not believing this was even happening. "I thought you loved me too."

"Lizzie, I cannot marry you. I lose everything, the people who rely on me lose everything. I could not care less about having nothing, but I do not want that for you. As for my employees, they do not deserve to suffer because of my father's spite and my inability to toe the line. I have to give you up, for I have nothing. I'm damned if I do and damned if I don't."

"You have shown lack of character when it was needed most. I will never forgive you for this."

"Lizzie, please," he begged, stepping toward her.

She held up her hand, halting him. "You don't even want me enough to try to find another solution. You've known of this predicament for a year and yet all you have done is taken the easy way out. Do not think for one moment I do not understand how important your estates are, the people who work both on the land and within your households, because I do. People need employment, a safe place to live. However, I also believe that fighting for love is important. I have never felt for anyone, have never allowed such intimacies with anyone else before in my life, such as I have with you. You're the man I wanted to marry, have children with, love and cherish for the rest of my life. But you're not willing to fight at all for any of those things. Instead you've chosen the cold and aloof Miss Fox and her thirty thousand pounds."

Hugo stared at her, offering no words, no excuses, or alternatives for how they could turn this all about. Lizzie shook her head, unable to believe that after all they had shared, they were even in this situation.

"Should I take a husband I want him to fight, not just for me, but for his responsibilities. A real man would've looked into every possibility he could to secure his properties, not sleep his twelve months away with anyone who would warm his bed. I'm just ashamed that I've enabled myself to be one of your many doxies."

She turned and he didn't try to stop her. She steeled her back, not wanting to know what that meant. She supposed it meant that they were really through, that he would marry Miss Fox and she would go home.

"I'm sorry," he whispered.

"Go to hell, you bastard."

LIZZIE MADE IT ALL THE WAY BACK TO HER ROOM AT HER COUSIN'S house before she crumbled into a fit of tears. At some point Katherine brought up tea and scones, but Lizzie didn't want any of it. All that she'd wanted was lost to her, and some heiress would claim the prize.

She had hoped, had prayed, that Lord Wakely would see her self-worth, not what her worth was to a marriage. How wrong she'd been. She had risked everything, had ruined herself by sleeping with him, only to have him discard her due to her lack of fortune.

She threw a pillow onto the floor. Of course she could see why he'd chosen Miss Fox. To be responsible for so many and have the threat that they would be left without any security wasn't anything even she would allow. But why hadn't he thought of another way? Like Lord Leighton had suggested, why didn't he look at other options so he wasn't left with only one: Miss Fox?

Lizzie didn't think she could ever hate anyone in her life, but right at this moment she hated Lord Wakely. Well, she would show him. If he thought she would skulk about London heartbroken, she would not. On the inside she might be broken, but on the outside she would be a rod of steel–strong, unbending, and hard. And no man, not Lord Wakely or any other, would ever break her in two again.

CHAPTER

SIXTEEN

Hugo wasn't sure what had come over him, but after seeing the hurt he'd caused to Lizzie, for the past two days he'd set about righting his wrongs of the past twelve months. That included a trip to his solicitors, and a hasty summons to the three stewards who looked after his various estates.

Tomorrow night was the Keppell ball, where for the first time since Lizzie had walked out of his life they would both be in attendance.

"Tell me again what isn't entailed and what I can sell. I know the properties are entailed, of course, but what's within them that I can be rid of? If I'm to marry Lizzie Doherty, penniless as she is, then I need all the funds I can get."

Mr. Thompson shuffled his papers and pulled out a list. "Between myself and your stewards, you could lease out Bellside Manor and Neverton Hall, leaving Bolton Abbey as your only country estate. At least for the next ten years. With the income those estates would yield, and if you gave the gentlemen who leased each property a lengthy contract to live there, the estates would be kept up and not fall into disarray."

Which would also see him save funds. "And the paintings? Which ones are able to be sold to a collector or museum?" Across all his estates there were numerous paintings, some that would have to fetch a hefty price. He would be sad to see them go, but not as sad as he would be to see Lizzie removed from his life forever.

The memory of her features crushed with hurt haunted him and would not dissipate. He shook the thoughts aside. He would fix this problem. What he'd failed to remedy in twelve months he would repair in two days.

"We were able to find six paintings: two large classical Titians, a Botticelli, a pair of Canalettos of Venice, and a Raphael portrait. I have offered them up to be auctioned privately, and if sold at their estimated value, they will almost put you back where you were financially had you never lost your mother's fortune."

"I never lost her fortune, my father simply gave it away," he reminded the steward. "And the London townhouse? Would I have to lease that out also?" Hugo asked.

"We've looked at the sums, and if you agreed to lease it out every second Season, it would place you in a more solid position. You have fourteen carriages across the three estates that you could sell, and the horses of course. If you were willing to part with them."

"Leave enough cattle for the carriages and servants to use, my hack of course, and the new carriage I recently purchased, otherwise auction the horses at Tattersalls and sell everything else. We won't be needing them all," Hugo said, relief unlike any he'd ever known flowing over him. He would win Lizzie back yet, and now that he could offer for her without the burden of his staff and employees losing their positions, there was no moral impediment to him asking for her hand.

Sorry, Father, but you will not best me yet.

Hugo stood, shaking hands with his solicitor and stewards in turn. "I must apologize to you all for making you pull these figures and an account of my property within the time that I've given you. I will be a more attentive landlord in future, better than what I have been in any case. I intend to go on as I am now. A viscount in name and in character."

"Very good, my lord," Mr. Thompson said, smiling.

Hugo nodded and left them to their work. Now he was ready for the Keppells' ball. He just had one more call to make before the evening. One more loose end to tie up.

LIZZIE STOOD TO THE SIDE OF THE BALLROOM AT THE KEPPELLS' ball, Sally standing beside her, her friend's thunderous gaze fixed on the Viscount Wakely and his dance partner Miss Fox.

They made a beautiful pair, and Lizzie hoped they both tripped and fell over. With that lowering thought she schooled her features and smiled at Katherine, who stood a little distance from her, but always with a watchful eye on Lizzie.

The deadline for Lord Wakely to marry was nigh and it was rumored tonight that they would announce their engagement that evening. The end of July was only days away after all.

"I cannot believe he has treated you so poorly and then has the audacity to show his face in public."

Lizzie threaded her arm with Sally's and hugged her a little. "I was the one who treated myself with so little respect. I should never have done what I did." Not that she'd told Sally of everything that had occurred between herself and Lord Wakely. Not even Katherine would ever know how far Lizzie had gone.

Even so, she'd been a fool. She had been the one who had stolen into his home, seduced him. She shook her head, hating the fact that she'd looked like a desperate fool. If only she could tell everyone she was an heiress, a woman who would from this time forward make her own choices, mostly that of being a spinster. A cat lady who would relocate to Rome, as she'd dreamed.

As the dance ended, she caught Lord Wakely's gaze. She flicked her attention away and fought not to glance back, to see if the longing she read in his dark orbs was a figment of her imagination or was actually present.

"Look how cosy Lord Wakely is with Miss Fox's parents. How ill they appear. I swear if they were not distantly related to the Duke and Duchess of Athelby the *ton* would turn their backs on them."

Lizzie didn't bother to look. She didn't wish to see in any case. As for her friend's claims, she doubted that would occur. As far as the *ton* knew, nothing untoward had occurred between herself and Lord Wakely. There was no reason to turn their backs on him, and even if they did know, it was she who would suffer the scandal. She would be the one shunned and excluded forever and a day.

The next set of dancing began and Lizzie took a glass of champagne from a passing footman. Maybe if she drank a little more, this night would not be so painful to be a part of. The dancers went about the quadrille, but then a disturbance had them pausing and within a moment the orchestra stopped and all eyes turned to what was happening in the middle of the room.

The sight of Lord Wakely standing in the middle of the ballroom floor, absent Miss Fox, gave Lizzie pause. What was he doing? She frowned as it soon became obvious to all that his attention was fixed on her and no one else.

The weight of a thousand eyes turning toward her hit her like a club and she raised her chin, not wanting to succumb to hysterics over what Lord Wakely was about to do.

"If I may have your attention, ladies and gentlemen," he yelled over the exuberance of the guests. "There is something I wish to declare before you all."

"Oh dear God," Sally muttered beside her, and Lizzie completely agreed with her words. What on earth was he doing?

"Some weeks ago I met a woman who embodied all that I wanted in a wife. A woman of strong character and substance. A woman who made me want to be a better man. And at a time when I needed to prove my worth, I let her down. The words may not have been spoken, but I broke a promise to her, and to myself."

Lizzie felt Katherine's comforting hand as she came to stand beside her. Lizzie couldn't move, couldn't form words, even though her mind raced with the shocking reality of what Lord Wakely was doing.

"Many of you knew my father, and know that in his final years he and I did not get along. So much so that in his will he demanded I marry an heiress within twelve months of his death or I would lose my mother's fortune, which keeps my estates running. I have not fulfilled that promise as yet, nor will I."

The silence was replaced with gasps for a time. The *ton*'s attention turned toward where Miss Fox had been standing, but was now vacant. Had she gone home? Lizzie turned back to Hugo, unwilling to hope, and yet her body thrummed with the possibility he was about to choose her.

Her...over fortune...

Her eyes stung and she sucked in a shaky breath.

"I'm sorry, Lizzie Doherty, but I cannot live without you. And if that means we will live without luxuries, without grand estates and trips abroad, then that is what I want. For I want you. Just you and nothing else."

Lizzie let go of Katherine's hand and walked as steadily as her shaking legs would allow. She came to stand before him, meeting his gaze, unable to believe what he was saying was true. It was too wonderful, too much.

"Do you mean it? Really mean it?"

He nodded, cupping her cheeks. "I have found another way to enable us to marry. Your words to me two days past shamed me, and you were right to do so. I have not been thinking and I did take the easy way out. But it was not the only way."

Lizzie cleared the lump in her throat. "And Miss Fox? What of her?"

"I spoke to Edwina and, as I suspected, she held no tendre toward our union. She has released me, although she did state that because there was never really an understanding, she wasn't sure why I sought her opinion over my choice."

"I appreciate why you did it, and I'm glad you did. It was the right thing to do." His thumb brushed her jaw and she leaned into his touch, having missed it dreadfully.

"I love you, Lizzie. I love you and no one else." He paused, taking one hand and kissing it. "Marry me, my heart. Be mine."

Lizzie nodded through a flood of tears, then laughed as he bent and kissed her, the *ton* and the startled gasps all forgotten as they sealed their fate before them all. He picked her up, hugging her close.

"I do love you. I'm sorry, my love. Please say you forgive me."

"I forgive you." She hugged him tighter still. "I love you too. So much."

Hugo let her down slowly, then pulled her toward Hamish and Katherine, where they were standing with Sally. The smile on her cousin's face told her she would have no argument with him in relation to marrying Hugo.

"Before we celebrate with my family, there is something you must promise me," Lizzie stated, pulling Hugo to a stop.

"Anything. I'll promise you anything," he said ardently and without hesitation.

"That is all I want. Your promise for anything."

"You're being very secretive, Lizzie darling," he said, kissing her hand once again.

She shrugged. "All in good time, Lord Wakely. Good things come to those who wait. And I think we've both waited long enough."

EPILOGUE

Lizzie breathed in deeply the dry heat and the air that was fresh and warm. Under the Tuscan sun she lay on a blanket, Hugo placing an olive on her tongue every now and then as he read the paper beside her.

They had purchased the small chateau during their honeymoon, which was mostly spent abroad. And now, whenever the chilling, damp English weather became too dull and cold, they travelled to their Tuscan home and enjoyed all that it had to offer.

"I see Miss Fox is a widow only two years after marrying that decrepit old duke."

Lizzie grinned, rolling over to lean on Hugo's legs and use them as a pillow. "Katherine wrote to say that Miss Fox is not the least heartbroken at his death, and with an heir secured, she's enjoying widowhood very well."

"I should imagine she is, and how could anyone blame her? The duke was old enough to be her grandfather."

Lizzie shuddered and rolled over to straddle Hugo's lap. "You seem very interested in what Miss Fox is about. Do you regret your choice?"

Hugo threw the paper aside and hauled her hard up against him. "Regret my choice? Regret choosing the woman I love, even if she did lie to me about being well-dowered?"

She chuckled, remembering poor Hugo's face in Lord Leighton's library the afternoon after the ball at which he'd so publicly declared himself. The mute shock that followed the declaration of how much she was worth. Worth waiting for, he had said, and she had hoped he was right, for he was certainly worth fighting for.

"I'm so happy, Hugo. If I was to die right now I'd know I lived well and loved with all my heart."

He kissed her and she wrapped her arms about his neck, never wanting to let go.

"I love you too," he said when finally they pulled apart.

"I don't believe I actually said I love you just before, but if you insist, I love you too. Shall we return inside, husband?"

He waggled his brows and she grinned. "Are you going to love me some more if I say yes?" he asked.

"Maybe. You'll have to find out."

Just then the meowing of one of their children sounded and Lizzie reached down to pick up Puss, the pure black kitten that had wandered into their yard some weeks before, and who had fast become part of their family. She kissed the adorable ball of fur, smiling at the purring that was as loud as its meow.

"How many does that make now?" Hugo asked, patting the kitten.

"Seven in total, but they're good at catching mice, and they're no trouble. You don't mind, do you darling?"

He shook his head. "I don't mind, no. You forget you told me of your plans to become an unmarried maid with an abundance of cats. I can tolerate the little furballs if it's what you want, and I get to have you instead of spinsterhood."

"I think really I have gained a good bargain with marrying you, Lord Wakely. I get my cats, I have my Italian sky, and I have you. I want for nothing."

"Me too." He kissed her again and she sighed as he deepened the embrace before one little black paw touched their cheeks. They pulled away, both looking at the culprit who didn't like not being the centre of attention.

Ah yes, life was positively perfect. And tomorrow, when Lizzie wrote her monthly letters to London, she would write to Lady X along with Sally and tell them all her news, including the surprise that she was bestowing on Lord Wakely tonight, of another addition to their family, but this time, one that came without fur.

Thank you for taking the time to read *To Vex a Viscount*! I hope you enjoyed the fourth book in my Lords of London series.

I'm forever grateful to my readers, so if you're able, I would appreciate an honest review of *To Vex a Viscount*. As they say, feed an author, leave a review! You can contact me at www.tamaragill.com to sign up to my newsletter to keep up with my writing news.

If you'd like to learn about book five in my Lords of London series, *To Dare a Duchess*, please read on. I have included the prologue for your reading pleasure.

TO DARE A DUCHESS

LORDS OF LONDON, BOOK 5

After five long years trapped in the country, newly widowed Nina Granville, Duchess of Exeter, has returned to town to start over. But it was here she committed an indiscretion—one stolen night of pleasure—that would threaten all she holds dear if revealed.

. . .

Byron always loved Nina from afar—until the house party that turned his world upside down. Guilt saw him flee England's shores, and Nina wed to a man old enough to be her grandfather, but now the handsome rogue is back...and ready to claim what is his.

Yet Nina has kept a secret from Byron, one that could threaten their sizzling attraction and sever their longstanding friendship forever. With Byron's brother determined to reveal the truth, Nina must use her power in the ton to ensure her secret is kept safe. Even at the expense of love...

PROLOGUE

Edwina Granville, Duchess of Exeter, sat in a carriage on her way back to Granville Hall, a large and imposing estate that resembled a castle. With its impossibly high walls and turrets, and its location on top of a steep hill, the only architectural elements missing were towers and spiralling staircases. The building loomed over the town of Minehead, Kent and looked as superior as the duke she'd just married.

From this day on, now that their vows were spoken, this was her home. She looked back out the window and watched the church disappear from view, her parents still standing outside and greeting the few guests who had attended from London.

A rumbling snore sounded from beside her and she turned to see the Duke of Exeter asleep, his head lolling about and his mouth drooping as if he'd had a stroke. She sighed, having not thought this would be her husband at the end of her second Season, but here she was, a duchess and wife to a man who was old enough to be her grandfather.

Her stomach roiled at the idea of bedding him, but she would bear it, and she would tolerate it with a formidable strength, because that was her duty, what she'd been brought up to expect upon entering the marriage state. The carriage lurched as it started up the steep hill toward the Hall. Edwina, Nina to her friends, would play the obliging, attentive wife for one reason and one reason only.

Because anything was better than to be seen by the man she loved as a pitiful, sad gentlewoman who had lost her head with the worst outcome. She narrowed her eyes, fisting her hand in her lap as she recalled the reason she was in this predicament.

Mr. Andrew Hill, a gentleman who had made her believe she meant more to him than she truly did. A bastard and flirt if ever there was one, and a man whom she should've stayed the hell away from. But she did not, could not if she were honest with herself. And now she was married to a duke, would have his children and be an upstanding woman of rank whenever they travelled to town.

Nina supposed she should feel guilty marrying a man she did not love, but she could not. The leech beside her was only too willing to marry a woman so many years beneath him in age it ought to be illegal, but her money and her family made her too much of a temptation. So when he'd offered, in her desperation about being slighted, she'd said yes. The one saving grace, she supposed, was the fact that the duke already had a son. One who was older than herself, which made for awkward meetings, especially because his wife, the marchioness, hated Nina with more passion than she loved her husband.

Nina stared at the grey velvet upholstery seat across from her. The decision to marry the duke had been made with such haste on her part, she hadn't considered in depth what it really meant for her.

Her time in London would now be curtailed somewhat, due to the fact the duke disliked town so much and left the entertaining to his son. A silver lining, perhaps, to the awful situation in which she now found herself. At least she wouldn't have to face the man who'd ruined all her dreams, and her in the process. Wouldn't have to face Society and their snickering snide looks because she'd sold herself into a loveless marriage and to a man twice her age.

The way she had fooled herself that she would be different from her parents, that she would have a grand love match when she took her vows, now mocked her to her core.

Nina sighed, staring down at her fingers. She would miss her friends, and one more than most. Byron, twin brother to Andrew, the blaggard who'd taken what he wanted with no iota of remorse. A man who could up and announce his engagement to someone other than herself could never really have cared for her. She would miss Byron though. He had left for the continent before her wedding and she wasn't sure when she'd see him again. She hoped it would be soon, but she wouldn't fool herself. She would probably never see him again.

KISS THE WALLFLOWER SERIES AVAILABLE NOW!

If the roguish Lords of London are not for you and wallflowers are more your cup of tea, then below is the series for you. My Kiss the Wallflower series are linked through friendship and family in this four-book series. You can grab a copy on Amazon or read free through KindleUnlimited.

KISS THE WALLFLOWER

LEAGUE OF UNWEDDABLE GENTLEMEN SERIES AVAILABLE NOW!

Fall into my latest series, where the heroines have to fight for what they want, both regarding their life and love. And where the heroes may be unweddable to begin with, that is until they meet the women who'll change their fate. The League of Unweddable Gentlemen series is available now!

LEAGUE OF UNWEDDABLE GENTLEMEN

THE ROYAL HOUSE OF ATHARIA SERIES

If you love dashing dukes and want a royal adventure, make sure to check out my latest series, The Royal House of Atharia series! Book one, To Dream of You is available now at Amazon or you can read FREE with Kindle Unlimited.

ROYAL HOUSE OF ATHARIA

DON'T MISS TAMARA'S OTHER ROMANCE SERIES

Tempt Me, Your Grace

Hellion at Heart

Dare to be Scandalous

To Be Wicked With You

Kiss Me, Duke

The Marquess is Mine

Kiss the Wallflower

A Midsummer Kiss

A Kiss at Mistletoe

A Kiss in Spring

To Fall For a Kiss

A Duke's Wild Kiss

To Kiss a Highland Rose

Lords of London

To Bedevil a Duke

To Madden a Marquess

To Tempt an Earl

To Vex a Viscount

To Dare a Duchess

To Marry a Marchioness

To Marry a Rogue

Only an Earl Will Do

Only a Duke Will Do

Only a Viscount Will Do

Only a Marquess Will Do

Only a Lady Will Do

A Time Traveler's Highland Love

To Conquer a Scot

To Save a Savage Scot

To Win a Highland Scot

A Stolen Season

A Stolen Season

A Stolen Season: Bath

A Stolen Season: London

Scandalous London

A Gentleman's Promise

A Captain's Order

A Marriage Made in Mayfair

High Seas & High Stakes

His Lady Smuggler

Her Gentleman Pirate

A Wallflower's Christmas Wreath

Daughters Of The Gods

Banished

Guardian

Fallen

Stand Alone Books

Defiant Surrender

A Brazen Agreement

To Sin with Scandal

Outlaws

About the Author

Tamara is an Australian author who grew up in an old mining town in country South Australia, where her love of history was founded. So much so, she made her darling husband travel to the UK for their honeymoon, where she dragged him from one historical monument and castle to another.

A mother of three, her two little gentlemen in the making, a future lady (she hopes) keep her busy in the real world, but whenever she gets a moment's peace she loves to write romance novels in an array of genres, including regency, medieval and time travel.